The Wild World *of* Buck Bray
The Missing Grizzly Cubs

≡

Book One

Also Available

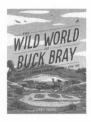

Text copyright © 2016 Judy Young

Cover illustration by Celia Krampien

Sleeping Bear Press™

2395 South Huron Parkway, Suite 200, Ann Arbor, MI 48104
www.sleepingbearpress.com
© Sleeping Bear Press

Printed and bound in the United States.
10 9 8 7 6 5 4 3 2

Library of Congress Cataloging-in-Publication Data
Names: Young, Judy, 1956- author.
Title: The missing grizzly cubs / Judy Young.
Description: Ann Arbor, MI : Sleeping Bear Press, 2016.
Series: The wild world of Buck Bray ; Book 1
Summary: Eleven-year-old Buck Bray travels to Denali National Park
to shoot a new kids' wilderness show, and with the cameraman's daughter,
they work to solve the mystery of two missing grizzly cubs.
Identifiers: LCCN 2016007682
ISBN 9781585369706 (hard cover)
ISBN 9781585369713 (paper back)
Subjects: | CYAC: Grizzly bear--Fiction. | Bears--Fiction. | Television
programs--Fiction. | Denali National Park and Preserve (Alaska)--Fiction.
National parks and reserves--Fiction. | Animals--Alaska--Fiction.
Mystery and detective stories.
Classification: LCC PZ7.Y8664 Mis 2016 | DDC [Fic]--dc23
LC record available at https://lccn.loc.gov/2016007682

For the Gleason kids,
who hiked up a mountain with me in
Denali National Park and Preserve

Your hiking buddy,

Judy Young

With special thanks to
John "One-Take Bake" Baker, an Emmy Award–winning director,
for consulting with me about cinematography,
and
Brady Baker, a conservation agent,
for sharing his firsthand experiences about crawling in bear dens
and darting hibernating bears.

J.Y.

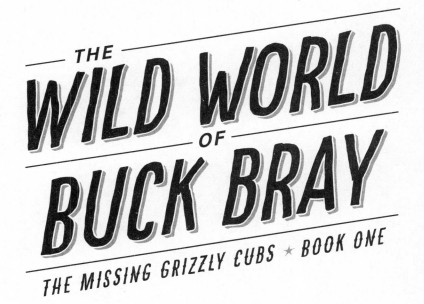

THE WILD WORLD OF BUCK BRAY

THE MISSING GRIZZLY CUBS ★ BOOK ONE

JUDY YOUNG

PUBLISHED BY SLEEPING BEAR PRESS

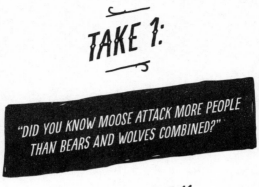

TAKE 1:

"DID YOU KNOW MOOSE ATTACK MORE PEOPLE THAN BEARS AND WOLVES COMBINED?"

SUNDAY, AUGUST 11

Buck knew he shouldn't be walking through the dense Alaskan forest by himself, but he and his dad had been driving for more than a week. When they finally reached a campground each evening, Dad said he was too tired to do any exploring. And each morning Dad was busy writing scripts. But Buck was ready for some action. He wanted to see a grizzly, but he wasn't going to see anything sitting in a camper all morning.

Buck hadn't gone far down the trail when he heard splashing noises. He quickened his steps. A swampy pond lay around the bend. His heart beating fast with anticipation, he sneaked behind a bushy willow and peeked through the leafy branches. It wasn't a bear, but Buck wasn't too disappointed. In the pond was a moose calf. It stuck its head in the water and came back up with strings of grasses slopping from its mouth. Buck smiled.

It looks like it's slurping green spaghetti, he thought.

Buck pulled his camera from his pocket and took some pictures. Then he stood perfectly still, watching the young moose eat bite after bite. Suddenly there was the sharp crack of a stick breaking behind him. Buck turned and immediately froze. Standing only forty feet away was the calf's mother. She was enormous. Busy eating leaves, she hadn't noticed Buck. Slowly, Buck raised the camera.

Although it was bright over the pond, it was dark in the forest, and the camera's flash went off automatically. The mother moose's head shot up. She looked straight at Buck. Then she looked at her calf. It was still in the pond. Buck was between the cow and her calf.

Uh-oh, not a good place to be, Buck thought.

The moose snorted and stomped, glaring at Buck. Buck

talked quietly to her, trying to calm her with his voice.

"You're okay, Big Mama," he said softly. "Don't you worry about little ol' me. I'm not going to hurt you or your baby. You just go back to eating your breakfast."

Again, the moose cuffed the ground with her hoof. As he spoke, Buck slowly backed up but hit a wall of willow bushes too thick to even crawl through. Little by little, he inched to the side, trying to put some distance between him and the agitated moose. The moose stepped toward him, easily covering ten feet in only two steps. Buck knew he shouldn't move, but fear took over. He darted behind the trunk of a spruce. Ears back, the moose lowered her head and charged. The spruce wasn't very big, and it didn't offer much protection from the thirteen-hundred-pound wall of muscle that came straight at him.

Suddenly the sound of their camper's door slamming echoed through the forest. The noise startled the moose. As her head turned slightly toward the sound, her shoulder rammed into Buck and slammed him violently into a tree trunk. Buck fell to the ground as the moose easily stomped past him, crashing through the thick wall of willows and into the pond. Splashing through the water, her calf followed her to the far side. When they stepped into the dense forest, the huge creatures instantly disappeared from sight.

"Buck, where are you?" Dad's voice came loudly through the trees.

"I'm right here," Buck called back, hoping his voice didn't sound as shaky as he felt. Buck got up and rotated his arm and shoulder around. Nothing was broken, but both were sore, and he could feel where big bruises were already developing. Buck took several deep breaths and strode casually up the trail toward the small remote campground, where the Green Beast was parked. Dad was walking down the trail toward him.

"I told you not to go wandering off on your own," Dad scolded him. "It's not safe to be by yourself in grizzly country. I had no idea where you were."

"I didn't go very far. But look what I saw!" Buck pulled the camera from his pocket and showed Dad the pictures. He didn't mention the encounter with the cow moose.

Dad looked at the camera. "Those are great shots, but a

moose can be just as dangerous as a grizzly. Especially a mother wanting to protect her calf. She could have killed you."

Buck knew the moose could have easily stomped him to death. He also knew if he told Dad about the moose's charge, Dad might have second thoughts about their venture.

———+———

Six years before, Buck's mom had died in a car crash. From then on, Buck had lived in Indiana with his grandparents while his dad roamed the far corners of the world, filming documentaries. Having a famous dad sounded exciting to all his friends, but to Buck it meant weeks and sometimes months without seeing his father. So, when Dad showed up after shooting the last episode of a series on Ancient Egypt, Buck was ready with an idea.

"The producers loved the proposal!" Dad told Buck. "They said having a kid as the star of a wilderness show was just what they were looking for. They want the first episode to be shot in Denali National Park."

"Wow! I can't believe it! I'm going to have my own TV show! And I get to go to Alaska! Maybe I'll finally get to see a bear!"

Dad was just as excited. "And you know what the best part is? I don't have to leave you behind. I hated not being around you for months on end."

"Me too, Dad," Buck said, smiling up at his father. "Me too!"

———+———

Now Buck followed his father back to the strange dark-green vehicle that was parked in the campground. The front half of the Green Beast looked like the cab of a military truck, and the back looked like a mix between a tank and a school bus. It had big heavy tires, propane tanks on the back, and solar panels on top. The words BRAY TRAVEL-ING FILM STUDIO had always been printed on the cab doors in big white lettering, but before they left Indiana, Dad had surprised Buck. Above those words, in fancy white letters, he had added the new show's name: THE WILD WORLD OF BUCK BRAY.

Buck stepped in through the back door and slid onto one of the benches at the kitchen table. Inside, the Green Beast was like an ordinary camper. At the front, Dad's bed stretched from side to side. The kitchen area was in the middle, and the table's two benches were the only places to sit. In back were two narrow doors. One closed off a tiny bathroom. Through the other, Buck could see pictures of bears tacked to the walls beside his narrow bunk beds.

"After breakfast we'll head to Fairbanks to pick up Shoop and Tony at the airport," Dad said. He handed Buck a box of cereal and pulled a carton of milk from the refrigerator.

"I know Shoop is your cameraman, but who's Tony?" Buck asked, pouring milk on his cereal.

"Shoop's kid," Dad answered.

"Oh," Buck replied, but couldn't hide the disappointment in his voice.

"What's the matter?" Dad asked.

"I thought I was the only one who would be on the show. How long have you known Shoop's kid was coming too?"

"I just found out this morning when Shoop texted me his arrival time. But don't worry. It's your show. Tony will be a gofer."

"A what?"

"A gofer. Someone who goes for stuff," Dad explained. "Plus, Shoop said his kid has a good eye with the camera and is great with audio too. We can use an extra hand, and you'll have somebody your age to hang around with."

"How old is Tony?"

"I think Shoop said grade six, so I guess eleven, like you."

Buck said nothing more until he finished his breakfast.

"You're right," he finally admitted. "It will be fun to have someone to do stuff with, since you're always working."

"Well, you know, I've told you. We're not on a vacation. It takes a lot of work to produce a show," Dad said, putting the dishes away. "So grab your scripts. It's an hour to the airport. You can practice while we're driving."

Buck moaned. "Again?" During the long days driving to Alaska, Dad had insisted Buck practice his lines. He had repeated the words so many times, he could have rattled off facts about Alaska's mountains and animals in his sleep.

———•———

The baggage pickup area at the airport was crowded, but there were only two kids who looked like they might be eleven years old. One was a boy standing at the far end of the baggage conveyor, his sweatshirt hood pulled over his head. The other was an Asian girl with a bright red backpack. She was sketching. A bearded man with a camo jacket and an identical red backpack stood near her.

"Is that him? The guy with the hoodie?" Buck asked. But before Dad could answer, the boy took a suitcase from the conveyor and walked away with a woman standing nearby.

"There's Shoop," Dad said, pointing toward a red-headed man standing beside the baggage conveyor.

As Buck followed his dad toward Shoop, he spotted another boy. This one was about six years old with bright red hair, and he was running all over the place.

Great, Buck thought, *Dad misunderstood. Shoop said Tony was six, not in grade six.*

"Glad you made it, Shoop," Dad said, slapping the red-headed man on the shoulder. "All your luggage get here?"

"It's all here," Shoop said, grabbing a hard-sided black case with a big scratch on it from the conveyor. He set it down by a heap of suitcases and bags near his feet, and turned to Buck.

"Hey, dude, you must be Buck. Nice to meet you. Go grab one of those luggage carts over there." Shoop dug into his pocket and handed Buck a bunch of coins.

I guess I'll be stuck with a hyper six-year-old, Buck thought as he headed to the far wall. He put the coins into the slot and tried to push the cart. Its wheels turned sideways and wouldn't roll. Buck discovered pulling worked better. So, walking backward, he pulled the cart toward Shoop. Not turning to see where he was going, he tripped over one of Shoop's bags and fell on his butt. Someone giggled behind him. Buck jumped to his feet and whipped around. Right in front of him was the girl with the red backpack.

"Hi," she said. "I'm Toni."

"You're a girl!"

"Very perceptive."

"Well, how was I supposed to know?" Buck said. "My dad said your name was Tony, so I thought you'd be a boy."

"It's short for Antoinette, and it's spelled the girl way, with an *i* not a *y*. Shoop's the one who came up with it. He says I don't look a thing like an Antoinette."

Toni was a little shorter than Buck, skinny, with long hair and bangs that hung over her eyebrows. About a dozen loop bracelets in all different colors were on her right wrist, a rainbow-colored watchband on her left. Every fingernail was painted a different color, and when she smiled, each band on her braces was a different color, too.

"You call your dad Shoop?" Buck asked.

"Yeah, everyone calls him by his last name."

"Yeah, but he's your dad."

"I know. But look at him. Does he look like a dad?"

Shoop was wearing a tie-dye sweatshirt and an old pair of cargo pants. He hadn't shaved for several days, and his chin was covered with whiskers a shade darker than the mop of bright red hair sticking out at all angles from his head. A small hoop earring was in one ear. Buck's dad was just the opposite: clean-shaven with short brown hair, his polo shirt tucked neatly into his jeans.

"Not really, but you don't exactly look like his daughter, either." The statement popped out of Buck's mouth without him thinking. As soon as he said it, he realized it wasn't very polite, but Toni didn't seem to care.

"Nope, I'm adopted," she said, and went back to her sketchbook, ending the conversation. Buck reached for the cart, but before he pulled it any farther, something caught his eye.

"What's up with that guy?" Buck asked.

Toni glanced up, shrugged, and went back to sketching, paying no attention to the man who was charging straight toward them, carrying a long hard-sided black case. The man's eyes were intent on Shoop's luggage, and for the second time that day, Buck was in the wrong place.

"Get out of my way!" The man shoved Buck aside as he rushed past. Buck grimaced as his sore shoulder rammed into the luggage cart. The man grabbed Shoop's case and dropped the one in his hand to the ground.

"You took the wrong case," the man said harshly to Shoop.

Shoop leaned over and looked at the tag on the case by his feet.

"Sorry," he said.

Saying nothing, the man hurried away.

"Awesome!" Buck said to himself as he stared after the man who disappeared into the crowd as quickly as the moose had vanished into the forest. But it wasn't the man Buck was admiring. Attached to the zipper pull of the man's red backpack hung a huge bear claw.

TAKE 2:

"AN INDIVIDUAL GRIZZLY BEAR'S HOME RANGE MAY COVER UP TO FOUR HUNDRED SQUARE MILES. THAT'S A PRETTY BIG BACKYARD!"

The two-hour drive from Fairbanks to Denali National Park seemed to take forever. To make matters worse, Dad had invited Toni to ride with them in the Green Beast, so Buck and Toni were buckled together in the only passenger seat.

At first Toni kept up an endless stream of chatter. Dad frequently added a comment or two, but Buck kept quiet.

Having a guy to hang out with is one thing, he thought, *but I don't like the idea of being stuck with a girl all the time.*

"Look at that!" Toni suddenly blurted out. "A bear!"

"Do you see it, Buck?" Dad's voice sounded excited too. "It's a black bear!"

Toni leaned forward to see around Dad. Buck tried to lean even farther forward to see around Toni, but the shared seat belt pulled tightly across his shoulder. All he could see was Toni's back.

"Move! You're in my way!" Buck complained.

"Sorry," Toni said. She sat back, but Buck didn't see anything. Just forest.

"It was on the side of the road," Toni said, "but only for a second. I barely spotted it before it darted into the woods."

Buck flung himself back in his seat, crossed his arms, and gave the floor a good kick. *It's not fair,* he thought. He had diligently watched for bears all the way through Canada and into Alaska. He'd seen moose and fox and even buffalo, but not a single bear. Toni had been in Alaska less than two hours, but she managed to look in the right direction at just the right moment and see a bear.

Buck looked out his window. The forest was giving way to rustic hotels and lodges scattered among a variety of restaurants. Gift shops advertised T-shirts, Native American jewelry, bearskins, and moose antlers. Outfitters offered a medley of rafting and fishing trips as well as airplane and helicopter rides that landed on glaciers. Buck gave up on seeing a bear. They drove through the small town and had just reached the far end when Dad called out.

"There it is," he said. "The entrance to Denali!"

At the side of the road was the big national park entrance sign. A mountain rose behind it in the distance.

"Is that mountain Denali?" Toni asked as Dad turned right onto the park road.

"No," Buck answered like it was the stupidest question he'd ever heard. "Denali is a lot bigger than that."

"Denali is the—" Dad said only those three words and then stopped.

"Now?" Buck complained, but rattled off the script. "Denali is the tallest mountain in North America. It's always covered in ice and snow, and most of the time it's completely hidden in clouds. A lot of people who come here never get to see it at all."

"I hope we do," Toni said.

I've seen tons of mountains, Buck thought. *I hope I see a bear.*

Dad pulled the Green Beast into a parking lot. Shoop pulled his rented RV in a spot beside them. In front of them was the Riley Creek Mercantile.

"We have to get our camping permits here," Dad said.

As Shoop and Dad talked with the park employee behind the counter, Toni and Buck wandered around the small store. There wasn't much there. Only a couple of loaves of bread, some cans of baked beans and soup, and a few other groceries were on the sparsely covered shelves. In one corner was a stack of caps with DENALI written on them, a handful of small souvenir pins, and three Denali T-shirts, all size extra-large.

In another corner were some compasses, canteens, and maps. Buck picked up one of the compasses, looked at the price, and dug into his pocket as he walked to the counter. Toni followed him, carrying a bag of marshmallows, the last box of graham crackers, and the only four chocolate bars.

"I got stuff to make s'mores," she said as Buck put his money on the counter. "I thought it would be fun to have a campfire tonight when it gets dark."

The park employee laughed and so did Buck.

"What's so funny?" Toni asked.

"In the summer, the days are really long this far north," the employee said. She looked at a chart taped to the counter. "Let's see. August eleventh. The sun won't set until ten twenty-four tonight."

"And even then, it won't get really dark until almost midnight," Buck added. "I'm still not used to going to bed before the sun sets or having it bright and sunny at five thirty in the morning."

"We can still have a fire; it just won't be dark," Dad assured Toni, and turned to the park employee. "Add three bundles of wood to the bill too, and I need a topographic map of the park and surrounding area."

"I know where they are," Toni said. As she hurried to the far corner, Buck followed Shoop out the door to where the wood was stacked. Soon Toni returned and handed Dad the map. Dad paid the employee, took the camping registration papers from the counter, and picked up the bag of groceries.

"Here, take these," the employee said to Toni. "There's information about why Alaska is called the land of the midnight sun in one of them." She handed three little booklets to Toni. Then she gave her three more. "Give this set to your friend."

Toni looked at the booklets. A blue one said *Junior Ranger Activity Guide for Ages 4–8*. A green one said the same thing except for ages nine and up. The third, an orange one, said *Junior Mountaineering Ranger*. It didn't have an age on it. Toni handed the blue ones back to the employee.

"We're too old for these," she said.

"Keep them anyway. They each have different things in them, and there might be something that interests you in that one too."

"Thank you," Toni said, and hurried out the door. As she followed the guys back through the parking lot, Toni thumbed through the booklets. Some pages had facts about the park's plants and wildlife. Others had information about dogsleds, hiking, and mountain climbing. There were drawings of animal tracks, photos of wildlife, and several different activities like scavenger hunts, word puzzles, and Denali bingo games.

"There's stuff about a compass in the orange book," Toni said, handing a set to Buck.

Buck took the booklets without a word but didn't look in them. *If I ignore her,* he thought, *she might decide to go with Shoop.* Concentrating on his new compass, he wandered in zigzags all over the parking lot. However, when Dad unlocked the Green Beast's door, Toni jumped in.

Buck sighed and climbed in after her. Before buckling his seat belt around them, he reached across Toni and dumped his junior ranger booklets inside a storage compartment between the two seats.

As Dad started driving, Toni opened her green booklet to a page with a map. Several stars on the map marked the park's campgrounds.

"Which campground are we going to?" she asked.

"Teklanika," Dad answered.

Buck glanced at the map on Toni's lap. Teklanika Campground was about a third of the way down the only road on the map.

"Why that one?" he asked.

"It's kind of complex," Dad said. "There's only one road, and it goes ninety-two miles into the park. The first fifteen miles is what they call the front country, and people are allowed to drive back and forth on that stretch. But at mile fifteen, there's a checkpoint, and only those camping at Tek can drive past that point. Tek is another fourteen miles into what they call the backcountry. That's the farthest anyone can drive. Once you're at Tek, your vehicle has to stay there, and you have to take shuttle buses to go any farther in."

"Buses? I thought a ranger would be driving us around," Buck said.

"Some of the time," Dad said, "but we'll be taking buses too. We want to keep our experiences as close as possible to what it's like for anyone coming to Denali. Anyone with a bus pass can hop on a green bus, go as far as they want, and get off where they want. To get back to the campground, you just hitch a ride with the next green bus that comes along."

The twisty road was steadily climbing, and wide valleys

stretched out to meet mountains rising in the distance.

"This is so beautiful," Toni stated.

"It sure is," Dad said. "I think Buck and I have worn the word *beautiful* out, we've used it so many times on this trip."

"Beautiful, awesome, gorgeous, unbelievably amazing," Toni said. "We could make a whole thesaurus about this place!"

Buck rolled his eyes, but Dad and Toni took turns seeing who could come up with another word to describe the landscape's beauty, counting each word as they went. Buck refused to join in and kept his eyes open for bears. Toni had counted thirty-eight words when they pulled up to the checkpoint. Beyond it, the road turned to dirt. Dad rolled down the window as a ranger came up to the Green Beast.

"Hi, I'm Craig. I've been expecting you."

"Nice to meet you," Dad said, reaching out to shake the ranger's hand. "I'm Dan Bray. They said you'd meet us here."

"I've been assigned to be your escort and have been

looking forward to seeing this monster in person," Craig said, looking up and down the Green Beast. "Pretty awesome ride."

"It's been all over the world, in some pretty rugged places," Dad said. He handed the ranger the registration papers. Craig looked through them.

"You'll need to write your name on this one and clip it to the post at your campsite. And this other one is your permit to drive to Tek. Tape it in the corner of the windshield." Craig handed Dad back the permits and a piece of tape.

"I know who Mr. Bray is; I've seen his shows," Craig said, looking around Dad. "But what are your names?"

"I'm Buck, and this is Antoinette," Buck said, grinning.

"I go by Toni, spelled with an *i*," Toni cut in quickly, elbowing Buck in his sore arm.

"Well, welcome to Denali. I'm looking forward to having some fun with you guys," Craig said, then turned back to Dad. "Let me see those papers again."

Craig shuffled through them. "Only you and Buck are registered with this vehicle. I'm going to have to call in to get Toni on the permit."

"You're in trouble now," Buck whispered, but Toni ignored him and leaned around Dad.

"I'm not with them," she told Craig. "I'm with Shoop. In the RV behind us."

Craig glanced toward the back of the Green Beast, a puzzled look on his face. Buck checked the side-view mirror. Nothing was behind them.

"Only one road and that man can still get lost," Dad said. He shook his head, but there was a smile on his face.

"Maybe he stopped to look at some wildlife," Craig suggested. "There's been a black bear in the area back there. We'll wait a few minutes."

It wasn't long before Shoop's RV pulled up, and sure enough, Shoop had stopped to watch a bear. Buck sighed.

"Everybody has seen a bear but me," he complained.

"Don't worry," Craig said. "Keep your eyes peeled. I'm pretty sure you'll see some. Farther into the park, a grizzly and its cubs have been hanging around pretty close to the road lately. And we've been keeping our eye on a male bear near there too."

Craig gave the side of the Green Beast a slap. "All set. I'll stop in at Tek this evening to go over our plans."

Dad pulled through the gate, Shoop followed, and they headed up the narrow dirt road. Although Buck's eyes scoured the surrounding landscape, he didn't see a single bear in the forty-five-minute drive from the checkpoint to Teklanika Campground.

Tek Campground had two loops. Dad circled counterclockwise through the first loop, slowing at each campsite that was not occupied.

"This place seems deserted," Buck said.

"Yeah," agreed Toni. "There are plenty of RVs and tents, but no one's around."

"They're probably all on buses for the day," Dad said. "Let's see what's in the second loop."

"How about that spot?" Toni asked as they turned into the other loop.

"Too close to the outhouse," Buck said. "It may smell. And you don't want the inside of the loop. Those sites aren't as private."

"I guess Shoop's not worried about it." Dad laughed,

looking in his rearview mirror. "He's backing in."

Dad continued driving. As the one-way road curved to the left, Buck called out.

"That's the one."

"The corner one on the right?"

"Yeah, it's got a lot of trees separating it from the other sites."

"I think you're right."

As Dad backed the Green Beast into the campsite, Buck looked out the window. A path just beyond the picnic table and fire ring led into the woods.

"Can we see where that goes?" Buck asked as he jumped out of the cab.

"Go tell Shoop where we are first," Dad said, "and see if he needs any help. Then we'll all go exploring together."

Buck and Toni raced each other up the road and helped Shoop get his camp set up.

When they got back to the Green Beast, Dad had sandwiches made.

"After we eat," Dad told Shoop, "I want to show you the scripts Buck and I have come up with."

"I thought we were going exploring," Buck complained.

"First things first," Dad said. "We'll go as soon as we can."

Buck sighed. "Can I at least check out the campground?"

"I don't know," Dad said. He was already looking through papers. He never even looked up.

"We'll stay together," Toni added.

"Okay," Dad answered, "if it's okay with Shoop."

"I'm good with it."

Buck looked at Toni. *I guess having a girl around is better than nobody,* he thought.

"And the path, too?" Buck added.

"Yeah," Dad said. "I checked it out while you were helping Shoop. It doesn't go very far. Just stay together."

Buck stuffed the last bite of sandwich into his mouth. "Let's go!"

The first place they headed was down the path.

TAKE 3:

"AS BIG AS THEY ARE, A CARIBOU'S ANTLERS CANNOT PROTECT IT FROM A POWERFUL GRIZZLY."

Just as Dad had said, the path wasn't very long. It cut a narrow swath through the forest and ended at the wide rocky bed of the Teklanika River. The glacial river was the same gray color as the rocks. It didn't even look like real water. The powerful force from the slow movement of glaciers ground up rocks and filled the water with grit, making it look more like liquid cement. Instead of stretching from bank to bank, the water rushed in narrow channels that intertwined and alternated with wide gravel bars. Buck and Toni stood on the bank a couple of feet above one of the gravel bars.

"I can see why the junior ranger book said the rivers here are called *braided rivers*," Toni said. She started to turn back toward the campground, but Buck jumped down.

"You shouldn't be going out there," Toni said. Buck ignored her and walked away.

"Didn't you hear me?" Toni said louder. "You shouldn't go out there."

Buck stopped and turned around. "What's the big deal? It's not like we'll get lost on a riverbed."

"What if a bear's out there?"

"If there was a bear out here, you'd see it."

"Not necessarily. It could be hiding."

"Where?"

"There," Toni said, pointing to a grove of willow trees growing on one of the gravel bars just upstream from them. "That's so thick, you can't see if there's anything in there or not."

"If you're so worried, we won't go that direction." Buck turned downstream. After a few yards he turned back to Toni.

"Are you coming or not?"

"I guess," she said, "but only because your dad told us we had to stay together."

Toni jumped down, and they walked to the edge of the first river channel. It was only about two feet wide, but the water was so gray, it was impossible to tell how deep it was. Buck squatted at the edge and reached in up to his elbow.

"It's freezing!" he said, and splashed water at Toni. Toni splashed him back.

"And gritty," she said, rubbing her hands together. "I wouldn't want to have to drink it."

They jumped across the narrow stream and ran to the next channel. The water in this channel was racing, wild and turbulent. It was way too wide to jump across. They followed the churning water downstream until they came to a long mudflat. It was the color of a dark rain cloud and looked really gooey. Buck stood in the gravel at the edge of the mud, bending his knees and swinging his arms forward and backward.

"You aren't going to jump in that, are you?" Toni asked.

"Why not?"

"You'll sink in over your knees."

Buck grinned at Toni, still bending his knees and swinging his arms.

"I'm not coming in after you if you get stuck," she warned.

Buck laughed and sprang as far as he could, but when he landed it wasn't gooey at all. It was almost solid, like wet sand. Buck stomped around and looked at his footprints. The soles of his shoes made a pattern of little triangles in the gritty mud. Toni joined him. Her shoes left rows of zigzags.

They continued walking downstream, sometimes on gravel bars, sometimes making tracks on mudflats. They had just run to another mudflat and Buck was mid-jump when Toni yelled out.

"Watch out! Don't land on them."

Buck's feet landed only an inch away from two different impressions.

"Wow! That's a bear print. Look at how long the claw marks are. It could rip you right open with just one swipe."

Buck slashed through the air with his fingers curled like claws.

"That other one's a caribou," Toni stated.

"How do you know? It could be a moose or maybe a deer."

"I bet you it isn't. I bet you it's a caribou."

"What are you going to bet?"

"A chocolate bar."

"I don't have a chocolate bar."

"Yeah, you do. I got one for each of us at the mercantile. You in?"

"In," said Buck. He pulled out his camera and took a picture of the tracks. Then he put his foot between the two prints and took another picture.

"You're going to lose," Toni said, squatting down to examine the prints. "First off, there aren't any deer in this part of Alaska."

"How do you know?"

"I read it in the junior ranger booklet."

"It could still be a moose," Buck said, shrugging.

"Nope," Toni said. "There are pictures of animal tracks

in the booklet too. A moose track is long and looks like an upside-down heart divided in half. Caribou tracks are more rounded, kind of a horseshoe shape."

Saying nothing, Buck quickly walked away, kicking at the gravel. But suddenly he stopped short.

"Toni, look at that!" he said, instantly forgetting his irritation at being tricked out of a chocolate bar.

"What?" Toni asked, hurrying to catch up.

About two hundred yards downstream, the riverbed turned to the right. Standing on a gravel bar was a huge bull caribou. It was stripping leaves from willow bushes.

"Wow! Look at the size of his rack," Toni said. Its antlers curved in a huge semicircle. "Have you ever seen a caribou before?"

"Not in the wild." Buck took out his camera, zoomed in, and clicked. "It's not paying any attention. I bet we could get closer."

"It says in the booklet not to approach wildlife."

"We won't be. If we go over to the bank, we can creep closer through the woods. It won't even know we're there."

"Okay," Toni agreed. "It's a few feet higher up on the

bank too. You'll be able to get a better shot."

Buck and Toni crept toward the bank, keeping the caribou in sight. The caribou didn't notice them as they sneaked closer through the cover of the forest. As Buck took more pictures, it continued eating leaves from one willow to the next along the near side of the wide band of turbulent water.

"Holy cow!" Buck suddenly cried out.

A huge grizzly rushed out from a thicket a little farther downstream and headed straight toward the caribou. The grizzly covered the hundred yards in just a few seconds, leaving the caribou no time to turn and run. The caribou put its head down in defense, its rack extending toward the bear. It charged, but its threatening rack did not intimidate the grizzly. The bear attacked. It forced its head between the lunging antlers and raised up on its hind legs, its front claws gripping the sides of the caribou's neck. The caribou continued its headlong charge. It pushed the bear backward into the rushing water, but the bear hung on and the caribou was pulled into the water too. It twisted and bucked over and over, trying to throw the bear off, water flying in all directions. But the bear hung on.

With each twist, each turn, each buck, the bear gained more control. Then, in one quick motion, it forced the caribou's head to turn, giving the bear just enough room to dodge its head under an antler. Buck and Toni watched, wide-eyed, as the grizzly clamped its teeth tight into the caribou's neck. The caribou bucked violently, but now the bear's weight was on top of it. The massive grizzly wrestled the majestic caribou down into the rushing water. Then, its teeth still biting into the caribou's neck, the bear savagely shook its head until the caribou's body went limp.

Buck thought the bear would let go, but it didn't. It easily pulled the dead caribou through the water to the edge of the gravel bar. Then, moving backward, the bear struggled to drag the heavy carcass halfway up onto the gravel bar before it started to feed.

Buck had been holding his breath the whole time. He had been so mesmerized, he hadn't even noticed that Toni had taken his camera from his hand.

"Holy cow," he said again. "Did you see how he hung

on? It was like watching a rodeo."

"Got the whole thing on video," Toni said, keeping the camera aimed at the bear.

"Look at him eating. He's just ripping the meat off of it. And did you see how fast he ran?"

Buck's words had left his mouth without thinking, but both he and Toni instantly grasped their implication.

"We'd better get out of here!" Buck said.

TAKE 4:

"A GRIZZLY'S FRONT PAWS CAN BE SEVEN INCHES LONG, ITS BACK PAWS ELEVEN INCHES. AND THAT DOESN'T INCLUDE ITS FIVE-INCH CLAWS!"

It was difficult to walk through the woods without a path. Buck and Toni soon had to return to the riverbed, but they stayed close to the bank. Frequently looking over their shoulders, they walked quickly back upstream. They carefully eyed every willow thicket and were spooked by each leaf that wiggled, worried a bear might charge out at them.

Alongside the river, the forest was a solid wall of spruce and willows. The two had walked for quite a long time, and now Buck's eyes followed the edge of the forest, searching for any sign of a small path that cut through the dense woods.

All the way through Alaska, the spruce forests had reminded Buck of the evil forests in fairy tales. Snow White, Little Red Riding Hood, and Hansel and Gretel wandered through forests like these. Forests with short thin trees crammed together so tightly, light could barely penetrate them. Forests where kids got lost. Forests where big bad wolves ate children. Buck knew those stories were make-believe, but the Alaskan forest was real. He was in a place where a bear really could devour a child. Yet he had not even left bread crumbs from his sandwich to show his way back. And worse, he had paid absolutely no attention to where he'd jumped down onto the gravel bar, how far they'd gone downstream, or how far they had come back upstream.

Buck glanced at Toni. She seemed unconcerned with finding her way back, but there was no way he was going to ask her if she knew where the path was. He looked around, trying to see something he recognized. There were willow thickets all over, but one just to his right was about the same distance from the bank as the one Toni had pointed to from the path. He looked intently at the riverbank. There was no visible path.

Remembering the compass in his pocket, he pulled it out. The needle swung around and stopped. It pointed downstream. *That's north,* Buck thought, *but it doesn't give me any idea of where the path is.* He wondered what the junior ranger booklet said about compasses, but he wasn't going to ask Toni that, either.

"Hey, look," Toni said, pointing behind them. "Who's that?"

Buck looked back just in time to see a man step up from the riverbed and disappear into the trees.

"Let's follow him," Buck said, a feeling of relief sweeping over him. Keeping his eyes on the spot where he last saw the man, Buck ran back downstream. Toni followed. Soon they both stepped up onto a path barely visible from the riverbed.

It wasn't the same path they had come down. The Green Beast was not at the end of it, but it did lead them back to Tek Campground. Just before the path entered a campsite, Buck stopped so suddenly, Toni ran into him. He grabbed Toni's arm and quickly pulled her with him behind a bush, out of sight from the campsite. Then he peeked out.

A small blue tent was set up on the other side of the picnic table. A big black car was parked in the drive. On the hood of the car sat a bright red backpack.

"That was him," Buck whispered.

"Who?" Toni whispered back.

"The guy on the riverbed was the same guy who was at the airport. The one who got mad when Shoop took the wrong case."

"How do you know?"

"That's his backpack."

"That could be anybody's backpack. It's a common brand."

"No, I know it's his. It has a bear claw hanging from the zipper pull. I wonder what he's doing here."

"He came to Denali. What's so mysterious about that? Lots of people come here." Toni started to walk out from behind the bush, but Buck grabbed her arm to stop her.

"He might be in the tent," Buck whispered. The tent's entry flap was rolled to the side and tied open, but the inner mosquito mesh was zipped closed. The mesh created a dark shadow, making it impossible to tell if anyone was inside.

"Who cares if he's in there?" Toni said.

"There's something suspicious about him."

"I didn't see anything suspicious about him. He just didn't want the wrong case."

"But he was staring at us at the airport. I saw him."

"Lots of people stare at your dad. He's kind of famous, you know. Come on." Toni jerked her arm from Buck's grasp, walked along the edge of the campsite, and stopped on the campground road.

Buck stared at the tent. Not seeing any movement, he left the bush, but instead of politely skirting the edge of the campsite like Toni did, he walked right into the middle of it. Scurrying between the fire ring and picnic table, he headed straight to the car. His eyes never left the backpack sitting on it.

"Wicked," Buck said as he closely inspected the bear

claw hanging from the backpack. It was black, nearly five inches long, and curved to a sharp point. A gold wire was wrapped neatly around the top and looped through the zipper pull. Buck reached out and touched the point, his mind replaying the sight of a huge brown paw with five claws easily ripping open the underbelly of the dead caribou.

"Come on!" Toni called out, waiting for Buck beside the campsite post.

"You need to come see this!" Buck said. "It's awesome. You won't believe how sharp it is."

"You shouldn't be messing around with other people's things," Toni said, but hurried back toward the car. She joined Buck, touched the tip of the claw, and then quickly said, "You're right, it is awesome, but let's go, okay?"

"Just a second." Buck snapped a close-up of the bear claw. He was going to take another photo of the claw lying across his palm when a voice yelled out behind him.

"Leave my stuff alone!"

Buck's head shot up. No one was in sight, but a man's voice came from behind the zipped mesh door. "And get out of here!"

Buck and Toni both tore out of the campsite. But as he passed the car's window, Buck glanced in. On the backseat sat the black case with the long scratch down the side.

"I told you he was acting suspicious," Buck said when they slowed down.

"No, he just didn't want you in his campsite," Toni said.

Buck ignored her comment. "He had the black case in the car. I wonder if a bear made the scratch on it."

"I doubt it," Toni answered. "But I do know one thing. Rek picked a bad campsite."

"Who's Rek?"

"Rek Malkum. That's the guy's name."

"How do you know?"

"It was on the tag on the campsite post," Toni explained. "And he has Site Thirteen. An unlucky number."

Lucky for us though, Buck thought but said nothing to Toni. *Number thirteen is in the first loop. So back on the riverbed, we walked right past our path and never even saw it.*

They walked out of the first loop, down the short stretch of road that connected it to the second loop, and entered that section of the campground without saying a word. The whole time Buck kept fidgeting with the camera in his pocket.

"We're going to have to tell them, you know," Toni said, breaking the silence.

"Yeah, I know, but Dad's not going to be too happy. He probably won't even let me step out of the Green Beast after what we saw."

"But we got a good video of the bear killing the caribou. Maybe that will help."

"Do you think Shoop can use it? My camera isn't a very good one."

"I'm sure he can."

When they got to the Green Beast, a ranger's truck was there. Shoop was standing at the far end of the picnic table, his camera equipment scattered all over. Dad and Craig were sitting on the bench, scripts pushed to one side and a huge map spread out in front of them.

"Hey," Dad said without looking up. His total attention was on the map.

"We saw a grizzly!" Buck announced. That instantly got everyone's attention.

"Where?" Craig demanded without any hesitation.

"Downstream." Buck turned on his camera and put it on the table. Everyone crowded around.

"Holy Toledo!" Shoop said when the bear first lunged at the caribou. They all watched in awe, but when the video ended, Dad was as angry as a bear. He jumped up from the table and roared at Buck.

"What in the world were you doing down there? Didn't I just tell you this morning how dangerous this country is?"

"You didn't say *not* to go out on the riverbed," Buck said. "You just said we had to stay together."

Every vein on Dad's forehead stood out as he tried to contain his anger. Shoop and Craig also looked furious.

"Your dad's right: you were in a very deadly situation," Craig said. "This isn't an amusement park. Wildlife can be extremely dangerous."

"We saw the caribou first and went back into the woods to watch it," Buck said. "The bear never saw us."

"That means nothing," Craig said. "If the breeze had been blowing the other direction, the bear would have smelled you long before you even saw it. And you would be much easier prey to take down than a caribou. But right now I need to know exactly where the kill was."

"Downstream, just before where the river bends to the right," Toni said.

Craig went to his truck, opened the door, and grabbed a two-way radio.

"We've got a situation here," he said into the radio. "A grizzly took down a caribou on the Teklanika, downstream from the campground where the river bends. Meet me there with a chopper." He put the radio back, then pulled out a rifle and a hard-sided black case.

"Are you going to kill it?" Buck asked.

"No, we don't kill bears unless they attack a human. I'm going to tranquilize it, and then it will be taken deeper into the park."

"Why?" Toni asked.

"Normally, we don't interfere with wildlife. That bear was just doing what bears do, but it's too close to the campground. It will be very protective of its kill, and if someone goes walking downstream, it could be deadly."

Shoop had his camera and was snapping in a battery pack before Craig even finished talking. "Okay if I tag along to film it?"

Craig nodded. Buck looked at Dad.

"Can Toni and I go too? Please?" he begged.

"You don't really deserve to go," Dad said in a sharp voice.

"This isn't the time for punishment," Shoop said. "He has to be in the shot."

Shoop turned on the camera and pointed it at Craig. Craig took a tranquilizer dart from the case. It had a long thin needle attached to what looked like a syringe. It didn't look much different from what the doctors used for shots, except the syringe had a bright orange end. Craig loaded it into his rifle.

"Okay," Dad said, "but mind what we say."

Shoop turned to Buck. "This is your first shoot, dude. Go get your shirt."

Buck peeled off his T-shirt as he raced into the Green Beast. He came out, buttoning a khaki shirt with THE WILD WORLD OF BUCK BRAY stitched over the pocket in green thread. From his neck hung a pair of binoculars.

Craig and Dad were already heading down the path. Shoop strapped on a belt with all sorts of equipment hanging off it. Light sensors, cables, and small round cases with lenses and filters in them all clinked against one another.

"Toni, grab the shotgun," Shoop instructed.

"You have a gun?" Buck asked Toni.

Toni flipped the latches on Shoop's hard-sided black case and took out a metal pole. She also grabbed a pair of earphones and put them around her neck.

"He's talking about this," she said. "A shotgun microphone. It telescopes out, making it longer. There's a mic on the camera, too, but this picks up sound better because you can aim it right at the source."

"How do you know all this stuff?"

"This is my first big project with Shoop, but I help him out all the time on smaller projects."

"Wow, you're lucky," Buck said. "I've never been with my dad on a shoot. I've only seen his shows on TV after they were all done."

Buck and Toni quickly caught up with the others. This time, as they jumped from the path to the riverbed, Buck looked around for a landmark. Seeing nothing that stood out, he quickly stacked several large rocks on top of one another near where they jumped down from the path.

TAKE 5:

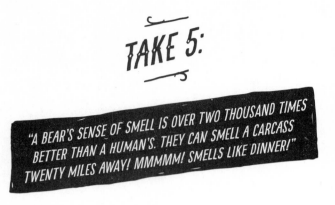

"A BEAR'S SENSE OF SMELL IS OVER TWO THOUSAND TIMES BETTER THAN A HUMAN'S. THEY CAN SMELL A CARCASS TWENTY MILES AWAY! MMMMM! SMELLS LIKE DINNER!"

They headed down the riverbed, keeping close to the bank. As they walked, Craig, Shoop, and Dad kept up a steady stream of brainstorming, but Buck scoped out the riverbed with his binoculars.

"There he is!" Buck exclaimed when he finally spotted it. Everyone stopped. Through the binoculars, Buck could see the bear was no longer feeding. It was pushing rocks and dirt up over what remained of the caribou carcass.

"We need to step into the woods. I don't want it to see us," Craig said. Everyone followed Craig up the riverbank and into the forest. "And remember, safety is number one. You guys can't get any closer. You'll have to stay here, way upstream. I'll need to get a little closer to be within this gun's range."

"No problem. My zoom is phenomenal," Shoop said.

"Is it safe enough to do a quick shoot with you and Buck out on the riverbed and the bear in the background?" Dad asked.

"From this distance it will be okay," Craig answered. "If we stay close to the bank and do it quickly."

Dad started directing. "Craig, just tell what the bear's doing. Anything you can think of. Buck, after he's done, I want you to add whatever comes into your head. No time to write scripts for this. Anything you need them to do, Shoop?"

"Yeah," Shoop said. "I know you won't shoot from here, but I want you to turn and aim your gun toward the bear. When I mix the shots, it will look like you tranquilized the bear from here."

Buck didn't say a word while the men were talking, but then whispered to Toni.

"What does he mean, mixing the shots?"

"It's like cut and paste on a computer. He rearranges shots so they're how he wants them to be."

Toni put on the earphones and extended the shotgun mic through the trees just to the edge of the riverbed. Dad held up a whiteboard out in front of the camera. On it, he had written, *Caribou Kill, Take 1.*

Shoop said, "Action."

Buck and Craig jumped down to the riverbed and looked back at the camera. A little red light was on.

"That grizzly has eaten its fill of the caribou and is now making a food cache," Craig started, "covering it up to finish eating later. Other than a sow protecting its young, this is the most dangerous time to come across a bear. That boar will kill to protect its cache. We're more than half a mile away. It's not safe to get any closer."

Shoop turned the camera toward Buck. Buck didn't hesitate. He knew exactly what he was going to say.

"You have to remember, we're not on top of the food chain here in Denali!" he said, looking straight at the camera's red light. Then Craig turned and pointed the rifle in the direction of the grizzly.

"That's a wrap," Shoop said. The camera's red light went out as Buck and Craig reentered the forest.

"I'll whistle when I'm about ready to shoot," Craig said, then slipped through the trees until he was out of sight. It wasn't long before Buck heard Craig's signal. It sounded like a bird calling. Dad held up the board again, this time stating, *Caribou Kill, Take 2*, and the camera's red light lit up again. Dad whistled back at Craig, and Shoop got ready with the camera.

Buck looked through his binoculars. He expected to hear a gunshot, but there was no sound. Instead he saw the grizzly suddenly flinch. It immediately stood upright on its hind legs and sniffed at the air. It let out a loud roar and, dropping back to all four feet, sprang into a run toward the bank.

"Holy cow!" Buck called out. "We'd better run!"

Buck had been so intent on the bear, he hadn't noticed Craig coming back through the woods to join them. Buck nearly jumped out of his skin when Craig reached out and took him by the arm.

"Stay still," he said. "Never run from a bear. Running sets up the bear's instinct to chase, and you can't outrun a bear. But you don't have to worry this time. The tranquilizer is taking effect."

The grizzly went only a few steps before it staggered and stumbled. It stood up again, wobbled, and then slowly sank to the ground, lying perfectly still.

"We need to wait a few minutes," Craig said, "before we go down."

"How come I didn't hear a gunshot?" Buck asked.

"It's an air rifle. It uses compressed gas and only makes a little pop," Craig explained as he reloaded the gun with another syringe.

"Are you going to tranquilize him again?" Toni asked.

"No. This is just a precaution. He should be completely out now, but stay here until I signal you," Craig said, then headed across the riverbed toward the bear.

As soon as Craig waved, Buck took off running, but Toni, Shoop, and Dad walked side by side, stopping a few feet behind Buck. Buck never saw that the camera's red light was on, the shotgun mic was aimed, and *Caribou*

Kill, Take 3 had been written on the board.

"Man, he stinks," Buck said. "Can I touch him?"

"Sure," Craig said. Buck knelt down and picked up one of the bear's paws, inspecting the claws and comparing it to the size of his own hand. Craig pulled up the bear's lip, exposing its teeth. Buck felt their sharpness and all the while, the camera recorded. Buck was still inspecting the bear when he heard the sound of a helicopter.

"You guys need to stay back," Craig warned. "It will kick up a lot of dust."

They moved away as the chopper landed on the gravel next to the bear. The blades slowed to a stop, but the motor kept running as two uniformed rangers jumped out. The one who was the pilot busied himself with hooking cables to the helicopter. The other took the bear's temperature and felt its pulse. He gave Craig a thumbs-up over the noise of the helicopter.

Craig called Buck over to help as the rangers brought a large net and spread it on the ground beside the bear. Together, Buck and the rangers rolled the grizzly onto the middle of the net. Then they walked downstream to the caribou carcass. They shoved it into the river and watched it float away.

Craig and Buck stood aside as the rangers climbed back into the helicopter. The blades began turning. The chopper slowly rose straight up until the net holding the sleeping bear swung above the ground. As it moved forward and upward, the camera continued capturing the helicopter until it was out of sight. Then Shoop turned the camera toward Buck. Toni had the shotgun mic aimed toward him too. They stood and waited, but Buck didn't say a word.

"Why did you push the caribou into the river?" Shoop finally said.

Oh, I get it, Buck thought. *He's cueing me in to say something he can edit into the shot.*

Buck looked at the camera's red light. "We don't want another bear to come in, smelling the kill."

When the camera's light went out, Buck went over to Toni.

"Why didn't you come over and touch the bear?" he asked her. "Were you afraid?"

"No. Shoop taught me long ago that when you're on a shoot, the crew has to stay on the sidelines," she said. "I wish I could have, but that's just part of the job."

"That stinks," Buck said.

They walked back upstream, Buck and Craig a little ahead of the others. As they walked, Buck reached into his pocket.

"Do you know how to use a compass?" Buck asked, pulling his compass out.

"Sure," said Craig. He started explaining, but Buck interrupted him.

"I know how to tell which direction I'm going, but what if you're trying to find your way back to where you started?"

"Good question. First, whenever you're in the wilderness you must be observant and keep a constant lookout for landmarks to watch for when you return. And if it all looks pretty much the same, you can make a cairn like you did."

Buck was surprised. He didn't think anyone saw him pile up the rocks near the path.

"It would be pretty scary if you couldn't find your way back, wouldn't it?" Craig said, giving Buck a knowing look.

"Yeah, but I still don't see what good a compass is, though. Not if you want to get to a specific spot."

"To really use a compass, you need to have a map. It's not that complex to learn, but it takes a little time. And it's best to learn by actually doing it in a real situation."

They had come to the cairn and waited for the rest to catch up.

"On Wednesday there's a class on using a map and compass," Craig told them as they stepped up onto the path and headed toward the campsite. "Want me to sign everybody up?"

"Sure!" Buck and Toni said in unison.

Dad wasn't so enthused. "I don't think we'll have time. We'll be doing a lot of shooting the next two days. On Wednesday we'll have to start editing and mixing, and—"

"Toni and I could go by ourselves," Buck interrupted. "We promise we'll stay together, won't we, Toni?"

Toni nodded, but Dad shook his head. "I don't think so, not after your escapades today." Dad sounded like his decision was final, but Craig spoke up.

"You don't have to worry. They can take the bus to the Eielson Center. That's where the class is. Bus drivers won't let two kids off in the middle of nowhere by themselves, and I'll have a volunteer go out to the bus when they get there. She'll make sure they get on a bus to come back, too."

Now Shoop piped up. "At least the class will give the kids something to keep them out of trouble while we're tied up with work. And if Toni takes a camera, she might get a few shots we could use for filler."

"Okay, I guess so," Dad said. "But you have to promise to stay together."

"And no going off on your own," Craig added.

"Promise," both Buck and Toni eagerly agreed. Back at the campsite, Craig went to his truck to radio in the reservation.

"Okay," Craig said when he returned, "you're all signed up. You need to catch the second bus Wednesday morning. It will be here at seven forty. You'll be gone most of the day, so bring lunch and plenty of water, and throw a jacket into your daypacks too. Weather can change suddenly in the mountains. But now we need to make plans for tomorrow's filming."

They all sat down at the picnic table.

"Because I darted a bear, I'll have to do some paperwork in the morning. So instead of me picking you up, you'll need to take the first bus at seven twenty-five. Tell the driver to stop at the Stony Dome overlook, and I'll meet you there. I'll be able to escort you around the rest of the day, but I think you'll be able to get some great shots near Stony Dome."

Craig looked across the table at Buck and smiled. "That grizzly sow with twin cubs I told you about? Well, she's been hanging around not too far from that area," he continued, "and that male bear is around there too. We've been keeping our eye on him, concerned he may be getting too close to the cubs."

"What difference would that make?" Toni asked.

"Male bears have been known to kill cubs," Buck quickly answered. That fact was in one of his scripts.

"What if we see some wildlife before we get to the overlook?" Shoop asked. "Can we get off the bus and film it?"

"No. The bus drivers always stop to look at wildlife and you can take pictures through the window, but nobody can get off a bus if animals can be seen nearby. They'll let you off anywhere you want if wildlife isn't obviously present. But for tomorrow, don't get off someplace and wander around. You won't have time."

"Sounds like a plan," Dad said.

"Okay. See you guys tomorrow," Craig said, and headed for his truck. He got in and started the engine, but before he drove away, he called out the window, "Don't forget to bring that map with you tomorrow. We might need it."

As Dad and Shoop looked over the scripts one last time, Toni put the camera equipment away. Buck folded the map and tucked it into a pocket of the camera bag. That evening the four of them sat around the campfire, talking excitedly about the caribou kill and the first shot of the new show. It was late when Shoop and Toni walked up the road to their RV, but when Buck finally laid his head on his pillow, he had a hard time getting to sleep in the broad daylight.

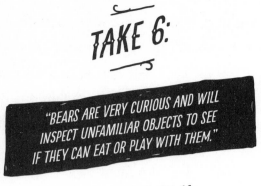

TAKE 6:

"BEARS ARE VERY CURIOUS AND WILL INSPECT UNFAMILIAR OBJECTS TO SEE IF THEY CAN EAT OR PLAY WITH THEM."

MONDAY, AUGUST 12

Early the next morning Buck and Toni led the way as Dad and Shoop hauled their gear to the covered bus stop at the campground entrance. Other campers were there, talking excitedly in anticipation of what they might see, but when the foursome arrived, their attention turned to them.

Many recognized Dad. Shoop and Toni backed away as a crowd gathered around him and Buck. Dad answered questions about the new show, introducing Buck as the star. As a green bus pulled up, Buck looked beyond the crowd. Standing to the side, Shoop had the camera aimed toward him. The red light blinked then turned black.

"You were filming me?" Buck asked as Shoop and Toni rejoined them.

Shoop grinned. "Promo shots, dude," he said as the bus driver opened the door and stepped out.

"Hi, I'm Jerry," the driver said. "You must be the Bray crew. I saved the front seat for you. It's the best seat in the house. Most of the mountain views will be out the left, and you'll be able to look out the front window and the door with unobstructed views."

"Thanks," Dad said as they got onto the bus. Dad stowed their equipment in the racks above the seat as Shoop sat down with the camera.

"The second-best seat is the last on the left," Jerry whispered to Buck and Toni before he turned back to board the other people.

The bus was already nearly full with campers from the front country campgrounds who had been riding for over an hour already. Buck headed to the back. The last seat had a clear view not only out the side but out the back window, too.

As he slid in, Toni pulled her sketchbook from her backpack, tossed her backpack up onto the rack, and sat down. She flipped through several pages until she came to a half-finished bird. *Willow Ptarmigan, Alaska State Bird* was written at the top. Buck watched as Toni drew.

"That's really good," Buck said.

"Thanks," Toni replied. "Shoop's teaching me about photography, but I prefer drawing. When school starts, I'm signed up for an art class. What about you? What do you like to do?"

"I don't know. I like science, and I know a lot about animals," Buck said, "especially wild animals, but until now all I've done is read about them. Dad's always gone, and the only wildlife I've ever seen is a squirrel when I've been with my grandparents in a park."

"Shoop told me you lived with your grandparents in Indiana," Toni said.

"Yeah," Buck said. "What about you? Where do you live?"

"Missouri," Toni said. "My mom is a professor there, but for the next year she's teaching in England. So that's why I'm here with Shoop."

"Are there bears in Missouri?"

"Some black bears in the Ozarks, but I've never seen one."

Toni went back to drawing, and Buck watched her as people boarded. As an older couple sat down in front of them, Jerry announced there was only one seat left. Buck looked past Toni across the aisle. A teenager was sitting by himself in the last seat on the right. Earbuds were in his ears, and his head was leaning against the window, his eyes were shut, mouth open, and he was sound asleep.

The people still standing in the bus stop pavilion were in pairs, and no one wanted to split up. Jerry was explaining that another bus would be along in about fifteen minutes when a man came running around the corner from the campground. Buck could only see the top of a black knit hat as the man ran by the bus windows.

"Are you by yourself?" Jerry said to the man.

"Yeah," the man said.

"You made it just in time. One seat left."

Buck was trying to get his camera out as the man

came down the aisle. It was zipped in the pants pocket by his right knee, and the zipper was stuck. He gave the zipper a hard tug, and it opened so suddenly, Buck's hand knocked into Toni's sketchbook. It flew off her lap and landed in the middle of the aisle one seat ahead of them. Toni stood and leaned over to pick it up, but the man was there before her. He kicked at the sketchbook just as Toni's hand reached for it. His boot plowed firmly into Toni's fingers. Toni cried out in pain as the sketchbook skidded under the seat in front of Buck.

Buck's eyes had followed the sketchbook, but now he looked up. The man had a beard and mustache. Large dark wraparound sunglasses covered his eyes, and the black knit hat was pulled down low, covering his forehead and ears. In the man's hands was a red backpack. A bear claw dangled from the zipper pull.

Toni stood frozen in the middle of the aisle, her left hand tightly holding the fingers on her right. Her eyes were as wide as if she were face-to-face with a grizzly.

Without saying a word, the man pushed past Toni, tossed his backpack up onto the rack, and sat down next to the sleeping teen. He put his head back and crossed his arms as if he were going to sleep too.

"Are you okay, honey?" the older woman sitting in front of them asked Toni.

"Yeah, I'm okay," she said quietly, but tears had welled up in her eyes. She quickly sat down and bowed her head, letting her long hair hide her face, but she still held tightly to her injured fingers.

"Do you want me to go get Shoop?" Buck asked. "It might be broken."

"No, Shoop's not too good with injuries, especially if there's blood. He faints. But it's not broken. See?" Toni let go of her hand and opened and closed all her fingers. Her little finger and ring finger were turning purple, and blood was smeared across them. The woman in front turned to look too. Then she got up, unzipped a side pocket on a big gray backpack on the rack, and stepped back beside them, holding a small first aid box.

"Let me see your hand, sweetie," she said. Soon Toni's fingers were cleaned up and bandaged.

"There. Does that feel better?"

"It throbs a little," Toni said, forcing a smile, "but yes, it's much better. Thank you."

"I'm Romana Rail, and that's my husband, Gerald." Gerald reached over the seat and handed Toni her sketchbook.

"I heard that your friend is Buck Bray, but what's your name, sweetie?" Romana continued.

"Toni Shoop. I'm the cameraman's daughter."

"Well, it's nice to meet you two. Now, let me know if you need any more help."

As Romana returned to her seat, Buck leaned near Toni and whispered, "Do you know who that is?"

They both glanced across the aisle. The man had not even lifted his head.

"Yeah," Toni whispered back. "It's Rek Malkum."

The bus had started moving, and as they crossed the Teklanika River Bridge, Jerry's voice came over the speaker.

"If you see some wildlife, just call out and we'll stop," he said. He continued talking, keeping a running commentary about what they saw and telling them other interesting facts.

Buck looked out the window as the bus started a long climb. The narrow road twisted and turned. The tires were only a few inches from a sheer drop-off with no guardrails. A braided riverbed lay far below. Jerry made a joke about how the park service had never lost a bus on this pass.

"They are always able to find 'em." He chuckled. "Eight hundred feet down."

The passengers groaned at the lame joke, but Toni whispered to Buck, "I'm sure that joke isn't helping Shoop any. He's afraid of heights. And I know the twisty road has made him carsick, too."

Buck chuckled. "No offense," he said, "but Dad's told me Shoop's scared of just about everything."

"Yeah," Toni agreed, smiling. "Blood, heights, snakes— you name it."

Buck stood up, looking over everyone's heads toward the front of the bus. Shoop was leaning over, his face in his hands. Dad had the camera and was taking shots of the treacherous pass through the front windshield. As Buck sat back down, he glanced again at the seat next to them. Both Rek and the teenager still looked like they were sleeping. Buck had barely returned his gaze out his own window when he saw something. Excited, he put the binoculars to his eyes and then yelled out the first thing that came to his mind.

"Animal! It's an animal!"

The bus stopped instantly, and everyone had their noses to the windows.

"You're right!" Jerry said over the mic. "Good eyes back there. Way down on that riverbed you'll see the first bear of the day. He's probably eating soapberries."

"I see it!"

"Where?"

"Over there."

Voices called out all over the bus. Most of the people on the right side of the bus were now crammed in behind people on the left side, trying to get a glimpse of the bear. When Buck turned to hand the binoculars to Toni, Rek no longer had his head back, but he wasn't even trying to see the bear. He was clicking different icons on what looked like a smartphone.

"We're a long ways from that grizzly, so it's not the best photo op," Jerry said. "We'll probably see more bears before the day's done, but when we stop for wildlife, you need to be as quiet as possible so as not to upset or scare it away."

The bus started moving again, and Jerry continued talking. "Now just up here, you're in for a treat. It's nice and clear this morning, so we'll get a good view of the Great One, which is what Denali means in the Athabascan language. It used to be called Mount McKinley, but in 2015 the United States officially changed it to Denali."

The bus went around a curve, and suddenly there it was. Denali loomed up bright white, twice as high as the surrounding mountains. A hushed *whoa* was whispered through the bus as it pulled to the side of the road.

"Take lots of pictures," Jerry said. "This will probably be the only time you see Denali today, from the looks of it."

Buck took some photos and then looked through the binoculars. Plumes of snow were blowing off the tall peaks. When he had woken up that morning, Buck had read the junior ranger booklets. Now he could see some of what the mountaineers had to face as they ascended to the summits of Denali's north and south peaks. There were narrow lines of jagged rocky edges where the snow was blown thin, steep ice-covered faces, and sheer drop-offs that climbers would need to avoid. And as clouds began to hide part of the mountain, any mountaineers up there would soon find themselves unable to see through a thick, freezing fog. Buck still had the binoculars to his eyes when Toni called out.

"There's a caribou!"

Again more voices, this time quieter. People pointed and clicked cameras. Buck found the caribou with the binoculars, then handed them to Toni, who in turn handed them to Romana and Gerald. At the front of the bus, Shoop was back at the window, his camera resting on the window frame, capturing the lone caribou walking across the tundra, Denali in the background.

"What's he doing?" Toni whispered to Buck.

"Filming, it looks like. I don't think he's sick anymore."

"No, not Shoop. I mean Rek."

Buck looked across the aisle and turned back to Toni.

"That's weird. He's brought a map up on his phone," he whispered, "but Shoop told me you can't get a signal in the park."

"Let me have your camera." Toni snapped a picture so discreetly, Buck barely realized she had taken one. Then she looked at the picture, zooming in on Rek's device.

"It's not a phone," she whispered, showing Buck the picture. "It's a GPS receiver. He doesn't need a signal. GPS receivers bounce off satellites, phones bounce off towers."

"Oh," Buck said, wondering if he'd missed that in the junior ranger booklets. "Why would he keep checking his GPS? He doesn't need directions. He's on a bus. Besides, there's only one road."

"The only time he sits up and pays attention is when animals are around," Toni said. "I think he's recording where they are."

As soon as the bus started moving again, Rek put his head back. Twenty minutes later the bus stopped so everyone could look at a herd of caribou grazing on the tundra.

"Those are all females," Jerry informed them. "Both

males and females have antlers, but the male's antlers are bigger. Females stay together, with the young. Mature males only come to the herd during rut."

Before looking at the caribou, both Buck and Toni glanced across the aisle. Rek was busy with the GPS again.

They had been on the bus for more than two hours when Jerry turned off the main road and entered a parking lot.

"This is the Toklat River rest stop," Jerry announced. "We'll be here twenty minutes. You can usually see Dall sheep on the mountainside across the river. That big tent is a gift shop, and on the patio, caribou and moose antlers are on display. Feel free to pick them up."

The aisle was instantly jammed with people. By the time Buck and Toni got off the bus, Dad and Shoop were already by the river, Shoop's camera aimed high at the cliffs. Using his binoculars, Buck spotted the bright white sheep with curved brown horns. They ran along very narrow cliff edges without any hesitation. He watched them for a minute, sharing the binoculars with Toni, and then headed toward the antler display.

"Come here, Toni," Buck called, holding out his camera. "Take a picture of me being a caribou."

"When I get back," Toni answered. "I want to look in the gift shop first before it gets too crowded. Another bus just pulled in."

Buck looked toward the parking area. A second bus had parked next to theirs and its doors were just opening. The first person off was a boy about Buck's age. Without hesitating, he came racing across to the antler display.

"Hey, I'll take your picture," Buck said to the boy, "if you'll take mine."

"Sure!" the boy said. Buck gave the boy his camera and then picked up the huge set of antlers attached to each side of the top part of a caribou skull. But he only got them to chest height before he put them back down.

"Man, those caribou must be strong to hold these things on their heads all the time," Buck said. "They're so heavy, I can't even lift them up to my head."

Gerald was walking by.

"Here, boys, let me help you," he said. Gerald lifted the antlers to Buck's head. Once Buck had them balanced,

Gerald stepped away and the boy snapped a picture. Gerald helped the other boy too and then wandered off to watch the Dall sheep.

"You're part of that film crew, aren't you?" the boy asked as they headed toward the moose antlers.

"Yeah, how'd you know about that?" Buck answered.

The boy pointed to the writing on Buck's shirt. "Our bus driver told us a kid is making a TV show in the park and we may see you filming some of it. Must be exciting."

"Not really," Buck said, shrugging. "What's your name?"

"Declan," the boy said. "I'm here camping with my family."

"Are you camping at Tek? I didn't see you at the bus stop."

"No, Savage River. It's in the front country."

They had reached the moose antlers, and they each picked one up.

"Wow," Buck said, "a single moose antler is heavier than the pair of caribou antlers were!"

As they took turns taking each other's pictures, Declan

announced, "Here come my little sister and brother."

Buck turned around and saw Toni heading toward them. A girl about Toni's height walked beside her, and a smaller boy tagged along behind.

"This is Anna," Toni told Buck.

"And I'm Liam," the younger boy said. "Can I hold that?"

"Sure," Buck said. He helped the younger boy pick up the moose antler, and Declan snapped a picture.

"We bought you some Beary Bites," Anna said as Buck put the antler back on the ground. She gave Buck and Declan each a package.

"And I found this for you too," Toni added. She handed Buck a small bag. Declan looked over Buck's shoulder as he pulled out a white sign with a silhouette of a bear on it. Bright red letters said: AREA CLOSED—BEAR DANGER. Smaller black letters read: ENTERING A CLOSED AREA OR REMOVAL OF THIS SIGN IS PUNISHABLE BY A FINE OF UP TO $500 OR IMPRISONMENT FOR 6 MONTHS OR BOTH.

"Where did you get this?" Buck asked Toni. "You could go to jail for taking it."

"I didn't take it; I bought it. The lady in the gift shop told me there are real ones just like it, except they don't have the stuff on the back." Buck turned over the sign. On the back was information about bears and about the sign.

"They really mean it about not taking the real ones, don't they?" Declan said.

"Yeah," Toni agreed.

"Thanks! It will look great with all my bear pictures!" Buck said.

Dad and Shoop were coming across the patio toward them. "Time to get back to the bus, guys," Shoop said.

Buck and Toni said good-bye to their new friends and raced each other across the parking lot. When they got to the last seat, Rek and the teenager were still there, both with their heads back and eyes shut. Soon the bus pulled out of the Toklat rest area.

Buck opened the package of Beary Bites and shared the bear-shaped fruit drops with Toni as the bus drove up one mountain, down the other side, and started across another bridge.

"Can I put this in your backpack?" Buck asked, tired of having the sign on his lap.

"Sure," Toni answered. She let Buck slide out of the seat. He pulled her backpack from the rack and carefully put the sign in it so it wouldn't get bent. As he was zipping up the backpack, someone called out, "Bears! Two of them. A sow with a cub!"

The bus quickly stopped at the side of the road. Buck dropped the backpack on the seat, and as he pulled his camera from his pocket, he saw Rek pull out his GPS device. Toni was already at the window, and Buck squished in between her and the back of the Rails' seat.

About fifty feet from the window stood a huge blond grizzly, head down, eating blueberries. Everyone was very quiet. Buck slid the window down to take a better picture. He could hear the bear pulling branches through her teeth, raking in the blueberries. She went from plant to plant, never even looking at the bus.

The cub was darker than its mother. It was standing on its hind legs, looking intently in the opposite direction toward a thick clump of alder bushes. Soon a soft chorus of *wow* and *awesome* quietly echoed through the bus as another cub stepped out from behind the alders. This one was the same blondish-gold as its mother. It was also eating blueberries. The dark cub dropped to its feet and charged at the golden cub. Together they tumbled and wrestled with each other. The mother paid no attention. She just continued eating, and everyone continued watching until Jerry finally pulled the bus away.

TAKE 7:

"DID YOU KNOW A GRIZZLY BEAR CAN EAT MORE THAN TWO HUNDRED THOUSAND BLUEBERRIES A DAY? THAT'S A LOT OF BLUEBERRIES!"

Craig was waiting for them at the Stony Dome overlook. When Buck stood up, he noticed Rek's GPS receiver was still on, resting in his hand on his lap. Rek's head was back again. Buck pulled out his camera and took another picture. When he got off the bus, he zoomed in on the screen and clearly saw a set of numbers and letters: 63°27′50″ N 150°12′28″ W.

Dad and Shoop were talking with Craig about the bears they had just seen. Buck showed the picture of the GPS reading to Toni.

"I know the *N* and *W* mean north and west," he said. "But I don't know what the degrees, feet, and inches marks mean."

"Craig will know," Toni said. Buck didn't have a chance to ask him, though. They all piled into Craig's truck and headed back up the road in the same direction they had come from. Craig stopped so far from the grizzly and her two cubs, they could barely see them.

"This is a safe distance from the sow and cubs," he said.

"We'll go up that hill. I'd like a shot in the tundra," Shoop said, pointing to the opposite side of the road. "Toni, keep the shotgun aimed. I want some covert audio."

Buck looked at Toni. "What's he talking about?"

Toni didn't answer. She put on the earphones but didn't seem to be aiming the shotgun mic at anything. It just sat cradled in her arms with its end sticking out sideways between her and Buck as everyone crossed the road.

"The tundra is so springy!" Buck said as soon as he stepped from the road. "Just like a trampoline!" He went from one rounded tuft of plants to another, bouncing like he was moonwalking.

"And look at the blueberries! They're everywhere!" Buck pulled off a handful in one swipe and popped them into his mouth. He kept eating handful after handful, juice pouring down his chin, until he was high on the hill. Buck scanned the bears with his binoculars. They were way below them and across the road. "They're still stuffing themselves with blueberries too."

"We might as well go ahead with the scripted blueberry scene," Shoop said. He handed Buck a kerchief. "Wipe your mouth off. You want to start with a clean face. Then pick a whole handful of blueberries but don't eat them. Stand over here, holding the berries out with both hands cupped like a bowl."

Buck cleaned off his face and gathered a bunch of blueberries. Dad added even more. He had so many, they were pouring out of his hands.

"Angle your hands just a little so I can see the berries," Shoop continued. "Good. That's great. Now look right at the camera and when I say, 'Action,' say your line about the blueberries. Then stuff all the berries in your mouth, look back up, and smile."

Buck got ready. His heart was beating as hard as when the moose had charged him. When they had recorded the first scene, he had been so excited about the caribou kill, he didn't have time to be nervous. This was different. This time he had to remember one of the scripts he had been practicing. *Don't mess it up,* he thought.

"Okay, you look good," Shoop said, peering through the camera. "How's the sound?"

"Buck, say your line just like you will when we shoot," Toni said.

He got halfway through his line when Toni interrupted.

"Too loud," Toni said. "Just use your normal voice."

Buck started his lines again. He got a few words out, and Toni spoke up.

"That's fine. We're good to go."

Dad held up the whiteboard, this time saying *Blueberries, Take 1.* The little red light came on and Shoop stated, "Action."

"Did you know a grizzly bear can eat over two hundred thousand blueberries a day? That's a lot of blueberries!"

Buck put his hands up to his mouth and crammed in as many berries as he could. With his mouth stuffed full and purple juice pouring down his chin, he looked at the camera, grinned, and said, "Mmmmmm!"

"Cut." The little red light turned off. "Audio?"

"No go," Toni called out. "I need a windscreen." She rummaged through her backpack, pulled out a black furry thing, and put it over the mic like a sock.

"We'll have to shoot it again," Shoop said. "Wipe your mouth off and get some more blueberries."

As Buck gathered more blueberries, he looked down the hill and across the road. The bears were no longer directly behind him.

"Should I move over there?" he asked Shoop. "You won't be able to see the bears from here now."

"That doesn't matter," Shoop said. "I've already got footage of the bears. When I get done editing, you'll see them down below you."

Dad changed the *1* to a *2* on the whiteboard, and they reshot the scene. Shoop checked the shot and said, "That's a wrap. Let's shoot the opening scene across the road. Those alders will be perfect."

Buck waited while Shoop and Toni set up. Then he walked slowly across the tundra, sometimes sneaking behind alder bushes and peering out, sometimes crouching low.

"Hi! I'm Buck Bray, and I'm in Denali National Park and Preserve in Alaska. I've just spotted a grizzly bear and her two cubs." Buck spoke very quietly as if he really were creeping up on a 450-pound grizzly and her 100-pound cubs. But in reality, the bears were almost a mile away.

They made a few other shots and then put the equipment back into the truck.

"I didn't know it would be like that," Buck told Dad.

"You can't believe everything you see on TV. There's a lot of manipulation to make things appear the way you want the viewers to see them."

"Could we get some audio on those bears eating?" Shoop asked Craig. "I couldn't do that from the bus, but I could hear them. It was incredible."

They piled into the truck. Craig drove slowly, pulling to the side of the road when they neared the bears. Shoop sat in front on the passenger side, camera pointed out the window. Toni sat behind him, the earphones on, holding the shotgun mic out her window. Buck sat beside her and Dad next to him. The bears never even glanced toward the truck.

"It's not that they're used to people," Craig informed them. "They really just don't give a darn. They're at the top of the food chain and they know it. With no hunting in Denali, they have nothing to worry about, and right now all they're thinking about is filling their bellies before winter. They'll be on a feeding frenzy from now until they hibernate."

As Shoop shot the bears eating, Toni pointed to the earphones and gave a thumbs-up to indicate she was getting good sound. The sow and the cubs were side by side. They walked parallel to the road as they ate, but the dark cub turned and wandered toward the truck. Shoop kept the camera pointed at the cub. Buck thought if the cub didn't look up soon, it would walk right into the side of the truck. The sow lifted her head and looked toward the cub. Suddenly the sow sprang up on her hind legs and roared so loud, Toni jumped and let out a little cry. Shoop gave her a hard look, and she quickly covered her mouth with her hand.

The cub turned to look at its mother but stayed beside the truck. Still standing upright, the sow made another loud roar, and the cub dashed back to its mother's side. The sow dropped back to her feet but gave the cub a vigorous spank with her paw. The cub bawled out, but the sow ignored it and returned to eating, moving farther away from the truck. Neither cub left her side again.

"That was awesome!" Buck said when Shoop finally put the camera down.

"It sure was," Craig said. "I've seen a lot of bears, but I've never seen one get after its cub like that."

"Did I mess it up, Shoop?" Toni asked. "Her roaring startled me. It sounded like she was right next to me in those earphones!"

"I bet!" Shoop said. "But don't worry, we'll have plenty of sound to work with."

TAKE 8:

"GRIZZLIES ARE GREAT DIGGERS AND CAN EASILY TEAR THROUGH THE EARTH INTO THE TUNNELS OF THE ARCTIC GROUND SQUIRREL IN SEARCH OF A TASTY TREAT!"

TUESDAY, AUGUST 13

The next morning they were eating breakfast at the picnic table when Craig pulled up in his truck.

"I've got an idea you guys are going to love! Buck, how would you like to go into a bear den?"

Buck's fork stopped midway to his mouth.

"Are you serious? I'd love it!"

"What if the bear comes back while he's in there?" Toni asked.

"No worries." Craig laughed. "It's an abandoned den, but it will require several miles of hiking. Will you guys be able to do that with your equipment?"

"Sure," Shoop assured him. "I'll take what I need and leave the rest in the truck."

It was several hours' drive, and they saw wildlife along the way, including the sow bear and her cubs, but they didn't take time to stop. Just past the Stony Dome overlook, the road made several hairpin turns, zigzagging sharply back and forth until it finally reached the bottom of the steep hill. At the bottom Craig parked at the side of the road. As they gathered their things, Craig pulled two canisters out from under the seat, identical to the one he always wore in a cloth holster on his belt. They looked like cans of hair spray, but stuck on the tops were trigger mechanisms similar to those on a pistol.

"Here," Craig said, handing one to Dad and the other to Shoop. "I noticed yesterday you didn't have any bear spray. You should always have it with you in this country."

"What about Toni and me?" Buck asked. "Shouldn't we have some?"

"I'm not comfortable letting kids have bear spray. People can get hurt if it's not used correctly," Craig said.

"When in bear country, it's best that kids stay with adults and not wander off on their own."

"I got the point," Buck said under his breath.

As Dad and Shoop attached the bear spray to their belts, Buck pulled out his compass. The article about compasses in the orange junior ranger booklet said to look for a distant landmark. Buck looked around. There was a mountain ridge with bumpy knolls on top that looked like knuckles on a fist. Buck took a compass reading. The knolls were in a south-southeasterly direction and lined up with the number 120 on the compass. Buck put the compass back into his pocket, pulled out his camera, and looked again at the numbers he took off Rek's GPS reading.

"Do you know what this means?" he asked, showing Craig the picture.

"That's a coordinate of an exact spot somewhere here in Denali, but I'd need a map or GPS to know exactly where. Why?"

"It's the coordinate of where the bear cubs are," Buck said. "I'm just curious about what all those little marks mean."

"You'll have time to discuss that at the compass class tomorrow. But right now we're never going to get to that bear den if we don't get started." Craig turned to Shoop and Dad.

"After we cross this valley, we'll follow that creek and then head up until we reach that bench," he said, pointing toward a small creek and then a flatter sweep of tundra. "Beyond that, out of sight from here, we'll follow a caribou trail that goes along a knife-edge. The den is on the far side of that mountain with the knobby-looking top."

Buck smiled when Craig used that mountain as his landmark too.

Toni pulled Buck aside. "Do you know what a knife-edge is?" she whispered.

"No, but with a name like that, I think we'll recognize it when we see it," Buck answered.

From the road, the valley looked like it would be easy walking, but it wasn't. They were waist deep in alder bushes that grabbed at their legs and scratched their arms. Craig led, avoiding places where the alders were over their shoulders.

It was also a lot farther across the valley than it appeared.

After thirty minutes they were only about halfway to where the land dropped down to the creek. Craig kept up a running conversation as they walked, quietly telling about the park, his various responsibilities, the animals he had seen, the mountains he had climbed. Suddenly he stopped.

"Freeze!" he commanded in a firm but whispered voice. "Buck, look through your binoculars. About a hundred yards out that direction, just at the edge of that ravine. There's an animal there, but I can't tell what it is." As Craig pointed to where the land dropped away, he slowly pulled the bear spray from its holster.

"All I can see is a brown patch through the leaves."

"Keep watching it." Craig took off the safety and rested his finger on the trigger of the bear spray.

Buck kept the glasses to his eyes. The brown patch moved, and he was able to see antlers, then its head and then its shoulder. "It's a caribou. It'll be walking out from behind those bushes in just a second. It doesn't know we're here."

"It won't unless it sees us move," Craig whispered.

"Let me see the binoculars," Craig, Dad, and Toni all

whispered at the same time. Buck gave them to Craig, who glanced in them for just a second before handing them to Toni.

"It's a young bull," Craig whispered.

Even without binoculars, Buck could clearly see the caribou now. It moved a few feet then stopped to graze. Shoop slowly brought his camera up. The caribou saw the movement. It stopped grazing, looked toward them, sniffed the air, took a few more steps, and then sniffed the air again.

"Don't move a muscle," Craig said. "We're downwind of him. He senses we're here, but he can't smell us."

The caribou was curious. It kept sniffing the air and coming closer and closer, then sniffing the air again. It was only about fifty feet away when it finally saw them. It turned and trotted away but only for a few feet before it stopped, turned, and sniffed the air one last time. Shoop was getting it all videoed.

They were watching the young bull when Dad whispered, "Hey, look over there."

Out of the same ravine, a female caribou came, followed by a calf. More and more females and calves came walking out from the draw, some crossing in front of them, others behind them. Soon the five of them were surrounded by dozens of caribou. They grazed, unaware of the people, and as they grazed they continued to slowly move across the valley.

The five of them stood motionless, watching, until the caribou herd had moved on past them. Even then they remained silent.

It was Buck who finally broke the silence. "It's a strange feeling," he said so quietly, he could barely be heard. "I felt like I was part of something that has been going on for centuries and not part of it at the same time."

"That's what I like about being in the wilderness," Craig said. "It's a mystical feeling."

"It made me feel really small," Toni added. "Did you know the caribou would be there?"

"There's an old Athabascan saying that no one really knows the ways of the caribou except the wind."

With that, they all continued walking, each with their thoughts. But when they reached the creek and started following it upstream, Craig quietly started talking again.

"It's a conundrum in bear country," he said. "You want to make noise as you hike so you don't startle a bear. That's why I talked all the way across the valley. But at the same time, you want to be quiet so you don't scare all the other wildlife away."

"In the junior ranger booklet it says you can wear little bells in bear country," Toni said.

"A lot of hikers do," Craig said. "Your jingly bracelets do the same thing. Makes just a little bit of sound to alert animals, but not enough to scare them away."

"What if that had been a bear back there instead of caribou?" Buck asked. "Would you have sprayed it with the bear spray?"

"Only if it charged us," Craig answered. "If that had been a bear, we would have immediately retreated."

They followed the creek for some time, and when the walls started closing in like a canyon, they climbed up over an embankment. They were higher now, and the alders had given way to the short spongy tundra. Still they kept going higher, their way steeper and steeper until they reached a point where the mountain dropped all the way around them. Mountain after mountain stretched out as far as they could see. Mountains that couldn't be seen from down below on the road.

Buck stood right at the top and stretched his arms out from his sides, twirling in a circle as he said, "I'm at the top of the world!"

"Get that on camera," Dad said. "Then we'll have some lunch."

Shoop put the camera down on the ground, took off his backpack, and pulled out an audio recorder and a little mic hooked onto a small clip.

"After I hook you up with this lavaliere mic, I want you to say that again, the way you did just now," Shoop instructed. He clipped the mic to Buck's shirt and hooked the recorder to his belt. Then Buck repeated what he said, twirling around again.

I'm starting to get the hang of this, he thought as he took a sandwich and scrambled up a large lichen-covered rock pile. A reddish squirrel with a short tail scampered out of the rocks and ran straight toward him. It stopped a few feet in front him, stood up on its hind legs, and proceeded to lecture Buck with a series of sharp little barks. Then it darted back into the rocks. A few seconds later it ran out from a different spot and barked at Buck again. It kept darting in and out of the rocks, letting Buck know how it felt.

"Hey, little fella." Buck was talking to it. "What are you all upset about?" As Buck spoke, his voice was still being recorded, and Shoop candidly captured the Arctic ground squirrel reprimanding Buck for being on the top of its mountain.

After lunch they continued on their way, following a caribou trail up and over another mountain. They were so high now there were just patches of tundra among bare dirt, solid stone, and crumbly shale. Ahead of them two steep slopes of crumbly rock met to form a long, almost pointed edge.

"That must be the knife-edge," Buck said to Toni. There was barely room for the narrow caribou trail that went along the top. The sides slanted away so steeply, one false step would have had them tumbling, unstoppable, for hundreds of feet. Buck couldn't even see where the bottom was.

"You have to take it slow," Craig told them. "Place one foot carefully at a time and, whatever you do, don't step off to the side. With that loose dirt and rock, you'll start sliding instantly. Do you kids think you can handle this?"

"No! No, no, no, no, no!" Everyone turned to look at Shoop. He had backed away from the others, and his expression looked as if someone had a knife to his neck.

"I've been handling this all along, and it hasn't been easy," Shoop said, moving his arm all around to show how high up they were. "But I'm not doing that!" His voice was in a panic.

"Calm down," Dad said. "I think you can. Just take it slow. I'll be right behind you."

"You'll be okay," Craig added, shooting a puzzled look at Dad. "It's not very far across, and the bear den is just beyond that." Buck looked at the knife-edge. It was at least half a mile across it, maybe more.

"Shoop gets a little spooked at heights," Dad explained to Craig. "Can he stay here?"

Toni turned to her father. "We can handle the bear den sequence, Shoop. You're just going to use the small head-mount camera and lavaliere mic, aren't you?"

Shoop nodded. And so it was decided. Shoop would stay and get shots of Buck as he went across the knife-edge and back. The rest of them would go on to the den without him.

Craig went across first to make sure the trail was secure, and then waited on the other side out of view, behind a little knoll. With Shoop's camera rolling, Buck tentatively put his foot on the trail. It felt solid. He slowly took another step and another, looking down one side and then the other. He was about a quarter of the way across when he carefully turned around and yelled back to Shoop.

"It looks worse than it is. It feels like walking on any trail, just no room for wandering." Then Buck continued across, making sure he placed his feet right where hundreds of thousands of caribou had before him.

TAKE 9:

"A GRIZZLY CUB IS BORN BLIND, HAIRLESS, AND TOOTHLESS. AND GUESS WHAT ELSE? IT'S BORN WHILE THE MOTHER IS SLEEPING!"

Buck stood with his back to a small hole dug into a protected corner of a mountainside. Holding the head-mount camera, Toni recorded Buck, who wore the lavaliere mic hooked to his shirt.

"It doesn't seem possible that a full-size grizzly could fit into a little hole like this," Buck said. He dropped to his knees as if he was going to enter, but then he turned his head to the camera. "But if a grizzly can fit, I guess I can too!" Then he disappeared into the hole. In a couple of seconds they could hear his voice echoing inside the tunnel.

"After sleeping all winter, when a bear comes back out, it's rrrrr-ravenous!"

Buck exploded out of the den, his teeth bared, his hands curled like claws.

"That's a wrap!" Toni said as they all laughed.

Toni put the head-mount camera on Buck's head, and he went into the hole again.

"Man, does it stink in here! Kind of a sweet musky smell," Buck said. Now no one outside could hear him, but the recorder captured his voice. He had crawled through the entrance of the grizzly den and down a short tunnel, and now the small light attached to the head-mount camera lit up the chamber. "There's not much room. Just enough for a bear to curl up nice and comfy for a long winter's nap."

Buck moved his head around, videoing the den's dirt walls. There were marks in the dirt made by the bear's claws when it had dug the den. Dried and decayed vegetable matter was scattered about the floor. Buck picked some up and let it fall through his fingers. "I guess it used the tundra for a mattress. Not much to choose from way up here above timberline."

He was just about to crawl back out when he stopped.

"Whoa!" Buck picked something up. He moved his head so the light shined on a big clump of thick brown fur.

"It might be a long cold winter up here, but wearing a whole blanket of this, you'd be toasty warm. Still," he said, moving his head around to shoot the den one last time, "I'd want a little decoration to the place. A little fireplace over in the corner, a couple of pictures on the walls, and a cup of hot cocoa would make this place a little cozier."

Buck crawled back out. Toni, Dad, and Craig were all sitting outside the hole, waiting.

"Look at this," Buck said. He still had the bear fur in his hand. He handed it to Toni.

"Wow, it's really soft," she said.

The clump of fur was passed to Dad, then Craig, and back to Buck, who stuffed it into his pocket.

"You can't keep that," Craig said. "It's illegal to take anything from a national park except photographs and memories."

"It's just a little piece of fur. What difference would that make?"

"Denali gets about a half million visitors a summer. If everyone took a little piece of something—a flower, a rock, or even a little piece of bear fur—the place would soon be picked clean. It's important to let the wilderness remain wilderness for everybody to see and experience. And that little piece of fur could line the den of an Arctic ground squirrel."

Buck pulled the fur from his pocket, but instead of turning toward the den, he turned toward Toni.

"Here, you take it back in," he said, handing her the fur. "You missed out on touching the darted grizzly. You can't miss out on going into a bear den, too."

"Thanks!" Smiling, Toni took the clump of fur and crawled in. When she came out, Dad took a turn going in the den too, but Craig said he'd already been inside.

Craig explained, "Late last winter we came up here to do some research on bear hibernation—"

"But bears don't really hibernate," Buck interrupted. "Sometimes they wake up and come outside in the winter."

"Yes, they do," Craig agreed. "But we're beginning to believe that bears do hibernate, just differently than other animals."

"So how are they different?" Toni asked.

"Well, for one thing, a bear's body temperature only drops about twelve degrees. Most hibernators' body temperatures drop much more than that. That Arctic ground squirrel you saw back there? Its body temperature goes down to twenty-six degrees during hibernation."

"Wow! That's six degrees colder than when water freezes," Buck said. "So when an Arctic ground squirrel says it's freezing, it means it!"

"I guess it does," Craig said, chuckling with the others. As Dad helped Toni put the camera equipment into his daypack, Buck looked toward the den.

"You said you came up here last winter?" he said.

"Yeah, this den had a mother and three cubs," Craig said. "We took their temperatures, listened to their heartbeats, recorded how fast they breathed . . . that sort of stuff."

"You went into the den when bears were in there?" Buck asked.

"We tranquilized the sow first to make sure she wouldn't wake up," Craig replied.

"You can't take a rifle in there," Dad said. "What did you use? A handgun?"

"No, a blowgun. That close up, getting stuck using a blowgun feels more like a mosquito bite than a mule kick. It's easier on the bear."

"Was the blowgun like what people in South America used with poison darts?" Buck asked.

"Pretty much," Craig said. "I went into the den while the sow was asleep, blew through the tube to release the dart, then crawled out real quick and waited until the tranquilizer had time to take effect. Then we safely entered the den and took our measurements."

"Holy cow," Buck said.

"You only tranquilized the sow?" Toni asked. "Those cubs we saw yesterday looked big enough to hurt someone too."

"Cubs are born in the winter and stay with their mother for up to three years," Craig explained. "The cubs you saw were already a year and a half old. But the cubs in this den were only a few weeks old."

"How big were they?" Buck asked.

"They weigh less than a pound at birth. The one I held wasn't much bigger than my hand."

"Wow," Buck said, looking down at his own hand. He was quiet as they walked away from the bear den, but when they reached the knife-edge, he turned to his dad.

"Do you think I could become a park ranger?"

"Maybe," Dad said. "Science and animals. It's right up your alley."

Shoop was right where they left him. He filmed Buck as he came back across the knife-edge and then told them that he shot some Dall sheep as they ran across the cliffy face of a mountain high behind him. He said he also caught an eagle on camera as it flew out from behind a rocky crag and soared right over his head.

"But mostly, I just sat here and marveled at that," Shoop said, pointing beyond the others.

"Marveled at what?" Buck asked, looking at several snow-covered mountains in the distance under the gray, cloudy sky.

"Sit down and wait," Shoop answered. "You'll see."

It wasn't long before the clouds started breaking up and they saw what Shoop had been watching. All the mountains surrounding them, as well as the one they were sitting on, suddenly became dwarfed by the presence of the Great One. The clouds raced past the enormous mountain, opening and exposing a face here, a ridge there, and sometimes the bright white top of Denali showed before other clouds closed over it.

"It's kind of like the wildlife around here," Buck stated when suddenly the mountain totally disappeared again. "Something as big as a moose can just step into the woods and disappear right before your eyes. You know it's there, but you can't see it. You wouldn't think a mountain that big could hide like that."

"Look," Toni said. "You can see it again. But just the top. It looks like it's floating out there, above those clouds."

They sat watching the mountain appear and then disappear, but finally Craig said they'd better get going.

"We still have a long hike back, plus a long drive."

"At least it's mostly downhill," Buck stated.

"And no knife-edges," Shoop added.

Buck hurried ahead and was soon in the lead. He recognized where he'd watched the Arctic ground squirrel, and was turning to go down the steep hillside when Craig called out.

"Wait up a second. Instead of retracing our steps, let's go back a different way. There's something I want to show you."

Craig went the opposite way around the pile of rocks. They followed him a few minutes up a slight rise and then stopped. Below them the land leveled out into a huge, almost perfectly flat expanse. The short tundra plants that covered the flat made it look as smooth as a blanket pulled over a bed. Another mountain rose sharply to the left.

"Wow, that's bigger than ten football fields," Buck said. "What made it so flat?"

"A glacier," Craig said. "Isn't it cool looking? You can't see it from up here, but at the far side there's a sheer cliff that drops off hundreds of feet into a ravine."

Following Craig, they made their way down to the flat. They angled across it and started up the steep incline to their left. About halfway up, they stopped climbing and skirted the side of the mountain. It was easy walking now, and Craig let Buck lead the way again.

A big rockslide edged the side of the short sparse tundra. It wasn't the loose gravelly rock like on the knife-edge and it wasn't anywhere near as steep, but large gray-and-black-speckled boulders were jumbled one on top of another down the side of the slope. The rocks were blocklike with flat sides and sharp edges, but among them, Buck saw something that looked out of place. Something the wrong shape and the wrong color, too. Something brown with a rounded edge. Buck moved closer.

"Cool! Look at this!"

Shoop instantly turned on the camera as Buck carefully climbed over some rocks and picked something up. When he turned back around to face the others, he held the curved shape of a Dall sheep horn to his head.

"Wow!"

"Let me see."

"Do you think a grizzly killed it?" Buck asked Craig, handing the horn to Toni.

"Probably not," Craig said. "Sheep tend to stay high up on cliff faces where bears can't get to them. It may have died from disease, old age, or even falling off a cliff. That happens sometimes. If a bear found a dead sheep, it would eat it, but wouldn't drag it far away. There is no sign of a sheep skeleton here. The horn was probably carried here by a wolf."

After everyone got a good look, Buck balanced the horn against a rock so it sat upright. He took a picture with the mountains in the distance and the valley below, showing through the circle of the horn.

"Lay it back down flat before we leave," Craig said. "If someone else comes along, they should find it the way it would normally be in nature, just like you did."

"Do rangers post where things like this are found so others can come look for them?" Toni asked.

"No, that would be just asking for trouble," Craig answered. "All sorts of people would be hiking up here, looking for it."

"What's wrong with that?"

"A couple of things. First, this spot wouldn't be so quiet

and peaceful. That's what this park is really all about. All sorts of space. Six million acres of it. Enough for everyone to discover what true wilderness is like for themselves. Not lots of people clumped together all in one spot."

"What's the other thing?" Buck asked as he rejoined them.

"Telling people where artifacts are may encourage someone to steal them," Craig said.

They started walking again. The caribou had all wandered off by the time they could see the big open valley below them. The truck was in sight, but Buck was so tired, he thought he'd never get down the mountain and back through the thick alders. Toni was dragging her feet too. As soon as they got in the truck, she rested her head against the window and shut her eyes. Dad and Craig also looked tired, but Shoop was wide-awake. He sat in the front seat, holding up his hands, his index fingers pointing up and his thumb tips touching, making three sides of a box. He looked through this box from one side of the road to the other, through the front windshield, and, turning in his seat, through the back.

"What's he doing?" Buck whispered to his dad.

"Pretending he's looking through a camera," Dad whispered back.

They had driven up the hairpin turns that led to the Stony Dome overlook and were now going down the other side when Shoop suddenly yelled out.

"Stop!"

Craig put on the brakes. Buck, Toni, and Dad all came to attention. Turning around and climbing onto his knees, Shoop leaned awkwardly over the back of the seat and looked out the rear window. "Look at that light. That light is perfect."

Everyone turned around. A large bull moose stood in the tundra near the overlook, yet it was easy to see why Shoop was more excited about the light than the moose. The moose's body blocked the sun, but a glow outlined the shape of the moose. Rays of sunlight coming from the broken clouds seemed to touch each antler point, looking like they radiated from them. The moose put its head down to graze, unconcerned about the truck, and the rays no longer appeared connected to the antlers.

"We might have one chance," Shoop said. "And we need to be quick or we'll lose the light. Toni, get the shotgun from the floor. Slowly, put it out your window. Real slow. You don't want to spook the animal. I'll shoot from the opened door. Buck, do you remember what you were going to say if we saw a moose?"

Buck nodded.

"Good. I want you to slip out the door on your dad's side, but don't close the door. The noise would spook it. Duck down so it can't see you, and go around the front of the truck. I need you to get between me and the moose. So as soon as you get around the truck and are hidden by my door, drop down and crawl to that rock with the orange lichen. Do you see it?"

Buck nodded again.

"The alders should hide you until you're in the right spot," Shoop continued. "Then slowly stand up. Keep your back to the moose, your eyes on me, and when I give you the thumbs-up, say your line. Don't whisper. Just say it in your normal voice. We'll only have one shot. We have to make it work. Okay?"

Buck nodded a third time.

"All right, then, let's go!"

Buck scrambled over his dad, slipped out the door, and crept, bent over. He peeked around Shoop's door. The moose was still there, grazing. Keeping his eyes on the moose, he crawled toward the rock but froze when the moose looked up. The big bull's ears twitched a couple of times. It took a half step forward but went back to grazing. Buck crept forward again. Even though the lichen-covered rock was only a few feet away, it seemed like miles. He could feel his heart beating rapidly, and he tried to stay calm. He finally reached the rock and looked at Shoop. The camera's red light was shining. Buck slowly stood up. Shoop cleared his throat. Not loudly but just loud enough. At the same time, he gave Buck a thumbs-up, and Buck rattled off one of the scripts he had practiced.

"The official state land mammal, the Alaska bull moose is the largest member of the deer family. Its antlers can span more than six feet from end to end." Then he stretched his arms out wide, like Dad had instructed when he practiced. "He's ginormous!"

Buck hadn't been able to see behind him, but when Shoop had cleared his throat, the moose had lifted its head, the sun had glowed in rays behind its huge antlers, and Buck had been captured on camera, stating his script. As Buck's arms had stretched out, the moose had trotted off, over the side of the hill, and was gone.

"Great shot! And just in time," Shoop said as a green bus drove past them. "I caught the light, and I'm pretty sure I missed the bus. How was the audio, Toni?"

"No go," Toni said with a sigh, the earphones on her head. She saw the disappointment on everyone's face. "Sorry. You can hear the bus, but it also sounded like a helicopter or something was in the background."

"Helicopter? Here?" Shoop asked.

"Could have been," Craig said. "There are a lot of what they call flight-seeing tours over the park. Which way did it go?"

"I didn't see it. I just heard it through the earphones," Toni said.

"The mic is real sensitive," Shoop explained. "It can pick up all sorts of things. Not a problem, though. Buck can repeat the line and we'll do a voice-over, syncing the words with the lip movements. The important thing is that I got the shot and it is fantastic!"

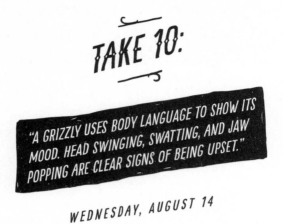

TAKE 10:

"A GRIZZLY USES BODY LANGUAGE TO SHOW ITS MOOD. HEAD SWINGING, SWATTING, AND JAW POPPING ARE CLEAR SIGNS OF BEING UPSET."

WEDNESDAY, AUGUST 14

The next morning it was cold and overcast, but Buck and Toni were excited about going to the compass class on their own. Again the backseats were vacant, and Buck headed straight for them.

"I'm glad Rek isn't on this one," Toni told Buck as the bus pulled away.

"Me too," Buck said. "I don't see anyone I recognize. We even have a different bus driver."

Just like Jerry had, this driver kept up a running commentary as he drove.

"Everyone is interested in the big five," he said. "Grizzlies, moose, caribou, wolves, and Dall sheep. I'm sure we'll see grizzlies, caribou, and sheep. Maybe even a moose if we're lucky. Probably not a wolf. They're rarely sighted. But I'm more interested in the little five: black bears, lynx, red fox, wolverine, and beavers. Actually, thirty-nine different mammals live in the park. We also have ermine, river otters, Arctic ground squirrels, snowshoe hares, hoary marmots, martens, mink, weasels, and pika, not to mention various kinds of shrews, voles, and other rodents, including one kind of mouse, a meadow jumping mouse, and one bat, the little brown bat."

From there the driver went on to list birds, then insects, and finally ended the list of animals with the only amphibian, the wood frog.

"In the winter the wood frog freezes solid. Its heart stops beating, and it doesn't breathe until spring, when it thaws out."

"I feel like a wood frog," Buck said to Toni. "I'm about to freeze solid."

The window just in front of them would not stay shut.

The people sitting beside it had tried to shut it, but just a little bump would send it sliding down again, the cold damp air blowing right into Buck's and Toni's faces.

Buck stood up to see if there was another seat open, but the bus was filled. So he pulled his backpack down from the rack and took his jacket from it. He handed Toni her backpack, and she pulled out a jacket, mittens, and a knit hat.

The driver had moved on to lists of plants, starting with trees. There weren't too many types, just eight species of spruce, willows, and birch. Then he started up on shrubs and flowers and then on to nonflowering plants. Buck and Toni looked out the window at the passing landscape. Having been up and down the road several times now, they recognized places and saw how Craig and the bus drivers knew where certain animals hung out. The big grizzly boar was spotted in the braided riverbed. Not at the exact spot as the other day but downstream a little ways. Although Denali was now behind clouds, the lone caribou that had stood in front of the mountain was still around. This time, though, it was walking near the road. A few miles farther a big herd grazed, but now the caribou were on the opposite side of the road. The Dall sheep could still be seen on the cliffs across from the Toklat River rest stop, where they had stopped before. Buck still couldn't lift the antlers to his head, but this time he also went in the gift shop with Toni and they bought some more Beary Bites.

"Just past this bridge is where the grizzly sow and cubs are," Buck said after they had left the Toklat rest stop.

"I know," Toni said, standing up. "Shoop already has a lot of shots, but I'll get the camera ready just in case." She pulled the small camera from her backpack and sat back down.

As they crossed the bridge, bright orange traffic cones were spaced alongside the road. Sticking out of them were signs like the one Toni had bought for Buck. About every twenty feet they read AREA CLOSED—BEAR DANGER.

"Those signs weren't there before," Buck said.

"I wonder what's going on," Toni said as the bus slowed slightly.

"There's recently been a grizzly sow with twin cubs in this area, but they're evidently having some sort of problem, so we can't stop," the driver said. "I'll go as slowly as possible. You may be able to see them. They're usually on the left."

They drove past three ranger trucks parked beside more orange cones. The rangers were all standing behind their open doors, binoculars balanced on the doorframes. One was Craig.

Buck looked across the tundra and spotted the sow not too far from where they'd first filmed her and the cubs. Now she wasn't calmly eating every blueberry in sight. This time she was clearly agitated, pacing back and forth and swinging her head from side to side. She stood up on her hind legs, just like when the dark cub had come up to the truck. She dropped to her feet again, made a short charge in the direction of the rangers' trucks, and then stopped, whacking at an alder bush with her gigantic paw.

As they drove on out of sight, voices throughout the bus speculated about what was going on with the bear.

"Did you see either of the cubs?" Buck asked.

"No, but I videoed the sow. Too bad we couldn't get audio."

"Shoop better be careful," Buck said, and smiled. "You might take over his place as best cameraman in the country."

"Camerawoman," Toni corrected him, smiling back.

The Eielson Center was about fifteen minutes past the Stony Dome overlook. As the bus pulled into the parking area, the driver told the passengers his bus would be at the center for about twenty minutes.

"Those wanting to take this bus back can leave their things on the bus. But if you want to stay here longer, make sure you take all your belongings with you. You'll be able to take any other green bus back."

Buck and Toni gathered their things, and when they stepped off the bus, a teenager came up to them. She wore an official-looking shirt and name tag.

"Hi," she said. "I'm K'eyush. You must be Buck and Toni."

Buck was not expecting the volunteer to be a girl only a few years older than he was, and missed hearing what she said her name was. He glanced at her name tag, but it was no help.

"It's pronounced *Kay-yoush*," she said, noticing Buck's look. "It means 'bear cub.' So you and I have something in common, Buck. We're both named after an animal."

"That's a pretty name," Toni said.

"Thank you. You and I have something in common too. Our long black hair and dark eyes," K'eyush said. Her voice was soft, with a pleasant songlike rhythm. "All things in nature are related in some way. When I meet people, I like to find at least one connection right away."

"I was expecting someone older," Buck said.

K'eyush laughed. "Craig didn't tell you? I'm sixteen. I'm here as a student conservationist."

"What's that?" Toni said.

"It's a pretty cool program. You get to come to wilderness areas like this and help with different things, like trail maintenance or wildlife habitat programs. I've learned a lot about compasses and map reading, so I get to lead the class today."

"Wow, that's totally awesome. I'd like to do that. How do you get to be a student conservationist?" Buck asked.

"When you get in high school, you can apply," K'eyush

answered. "I'll give you some information inside."

"Inside?" Buck asked, looking around. All that was there was the parking lot, a set of stairs, and tundra plants.

"The Eielson Center is partially buried in the ground, so you can't see it from the road," K'eyush said, "and with tundra actually on the roof, it blends in with the landscape as much as possible. On a clear day the view of Denali is magnificent from here. But obviously that's not the case today."

"Where are they going?" Buck asked, pointing behind him at a steep trail on the other side of the road. A stream of people was on it, some walking up, others coming down.

"There aren't many trails in Denali. A few in the front country and two here. That one goes almost straight up to the top of that ridge. And there's a shorter one down there, in front of the center. It's more of a nature walk than a trail, but for most people these are the only places they walk around in the park. Unfortunately, only a handful of people actually get off one of the buses and really experience being out in the wilderness."

"We have," Buck said proudly. "Yesterday we hiked

with Craig. It was unbelievable."

As they walked across the parking lot, down the set of stairs, and onto a patio, Buck told K'eyush about walking through the caribou herd, crawling in a bear den, and finding a sheep horn.

"Sounds like a great day," she said as she held the door open for them. "I hope you have fun in my compass class, too. I have some things to do before that, though. Will you two be okay in the center by yourselves for a little while? There will be an announcement when the class starts."

"Sure, but I have a question first. What's going on with the grizzly and cubs that hang out just before Stony Dome?"

Buck explained what they had seen, but K'eyush had heard nothing about it.

Buck and Toni wandered around through the Eielson Center. They flipped up little flaps on a display telling about wildlife and then looked at a large round, three-dimensional relief model of the entire park. Snow-covered mountains and glaciers took up more than half of the model. There was a marker that showed where the

Eielson Center was, and Buck and Toni tried to figure out where they'd hiked the day before. Then Buck wandered alone over to displays about mountaineers who'd climbed Denali, reading that the first people to ever reach the top did so in 1913.

After inspecting a wood frame backpack used by early mountaineers and a canvas tent they slept in, Buck went over to the big picture window. There was no view of Denali, just fog. To the side of the large window was a table filled with pelts. Grizzly, black bear, lynx, wolf. The furs were right beside a long counter, where two rangers stood ready to answer visitors' questions. At that moment no visitors were there, and the two rangers were talking to each other. As Buck stroked the furs, he could hear them plainly. He listened intently until a lady came up to inquire about restrooms and put an end to the rangers' conversation.

Buck looked around the large room. Toni was sitting cross-legged on the floor in front of a huge quilt hanging at the far end. She had her sketchbook out.

"Isn't this cool?" Toni said as Buck rushed up. "The

quilt has the whole mountain and all sorts of flowers and animals that are here in the park too. Since we can't see Denali today, I'm sketching it from the quilt."

Toni held up the sketchbook to show Buck, but he barely glanced at it.

"I have important news. The cubs are missing!"

"Missing?"

"Yeah, that's why the sow was so upset. She can't find her cubs."

"How do you know?"

"I overheard some rangers."

"The cubs were there last night when we drove by after the moose shot," Toni said. "They were all still eating blueberries. What do they think happened to them?"

"No one knows. One of the rangers said the cubs might have wandered off and gotten lost, but the other said sows keep pretty good track of their cubs, so that wasn't very likely."

"Remember how Craig said a male bear was hanging around that area? Maybe it killed them," Toni said.

"They talked about that, too, but said there wasn't any

evidence. If a boar killed them, the rangers would have seen the cubs' bodies or a food cache, but they didn't. They didn't see anything."

"What do you think happened?"

"I don't know, but I do know one thing. The cubs didn't just disappear into thin air."

TAKE 11:

"GRIZZLIES WANDER OVER LOWER ELEVATIONS DURING THE SUMMER BUT SEEK HIGHER GROUNDS TO HIBERNATE."

A voice called out through the room, announcing that those signed up for the compass class were to meet on the patio.

"I wish we could be with Craig today," Buck said as he and Toni headed out the door. "If he's still there when we go back, maybe we could get off the bus."

"They're not even letting the buses stop for pictures there," Toni said. "No way they'd stop to let two kids off."

"You're probably right," Buck said.

K'eyush was waiting on the patio. Because of the

weather, only a few people showed up. There were two older women and a young couple who spoke German to each other but understood English, too.

"Hey, Gerald and Romana are over there," Toni said. She and Buck headed across the patio toward the Rails.

"Gerald, it's our friends!" Romana said. "How's your finger, Toni?"

Toni held up her hand. "Much better. It's still purple, but the swelling has gone down."

K'eyush introduced herself and started handing out compasses to anyone who didn't have one when a man's voice called out from behind them.

"Is this the compass class?"

Everyone turned around. A family of five was hurrying down the stairs from the parking lot.

"Declan!" Buck called out just as Toni said, "Anna!"

K'eyush waited while the family came to stand beside Buck and Toni. "Welcome," she stated. "You're just in time."

As K'eyush explained the basics of a compass, Buck whispered to Declan, "Did you just get here?"

"No, we've been here for about an hour. We hiked up that trail on the other side of the road."

"So you were on the first bus. Did you see a bear with two cubs just after the Toklat rest area?"

"We saw a bear but not any cubs. The bear was really upset. We stayed there for a long time, and our driver radioed in to the rangers that something seemed wrong. Why? What's going on?"

"That bear has two cubs, but they're missing."

Buck started to explain more, but K'eyush interrupted. "Are you guys coming?"

The rest of the group had moved over to the table where K'eyush was opening a map and spreading it out. Buck and Declan hurried over.

"This is a topographical map," K'eyush explained. "See all those squiggly lines? They're called contour lines, and they show elevation."

"What's elevation mean?" Liam asked.

"How high up you are," Declan answered.

"Right," K'eyush said. "The closer together the lines are, the steeper the hill is."

"It must be really steep there," Buck said, pointing to a place where the lines were so close together, they were almost on top of one another.

"Probably there's a cliff there," K'eyush explained.

"See that line, the one that makes a little circle near the Stony Dome overlook?" Toni said, pointing out a spot to Anna. Declan, Romana, and Gerald leaned over Toni's shoulders to see where she was pointing. "It's really flat right there, and we found a Dall sheep horn in a rockslide nearby."

"Wicked!" Declan said, and turned to his dad. "When we get done here, can we go find the sheep horn?"

"That would be fun," Romana said to Gerald. "We were talking about hiking after the class. Maybe we should try there."

"Show us again. Exactly where did you see the horn?" the German couple said.

"Yes, where is it, honey?" one of the older women asked.

K'eyush interrupted everyone's excitement about the sheep horn as she started showing them how to lay a compass on the map.

"You shouldn't have told about the sheep horn," Buck quietly scolded Toni.

"You told first."

"No, I didn't."

"Yes, you did. You told K'eyush out in the parking lot."

"But I didn't point it out on a map. Now it will be just like Craig said. Everybody and their brother will be up there."

Toni turned her back on Buck as K'eyush continued explaining how to determine directions and coordinates.

"Couldn't you use a GPS device instead of a compass?" Buck asked.

"Yes, but even those who use GPS devices should have and know how to use a compass and map. A GPS device may tell you to go northwest at two hundred and seventy-three degrees, but it might not tell you that a cliff or a river is right in your path."

"Yeah, and your battery could go dead," Liam spoke up.

K'eyush smiled. "How old are you?"

"Seven."

"Well, you're absolutely right," K'eyush said. "So we're

going to play a game to learn how to use less technology and become more self-reliant. First, I want you to get in teams."

K'eyush handed several laminated maps to Liam. "Here, give one to each team." As Liam handed out the maps, K'eyush continued, "Use your compass to follow the coordinates on the back of your map. Don't just follow another team. You should all end up in different places."

Buck and Declan finished at the flagpole on the patio. Toni and Anna ended at the picnic table. Liam and his parents were near the entrance doors. The German couple stood on the stairs, and Romana and Gerald were coming toward the patio from another direction. When the two older women reached their destination, K'eyush called everyone back to the picnic table.

"It looks like everybody ended up where they were supposed to," she said. "And I have a special award for Liam. A junior ranger badge for being the youngest in the group to complete the compass course." As K'eyush pinned a gold badge, similar to the ones the rangers wore, on Liam's shirt, Buck pulled Declan, Toni, and Anna aside.

"Declan, why don't you and Anna talk your parents into going hiking to the sheep horn, and Toni and I will show you the way?"

"That sounds great!" Declan exclaimed, and he and Anna rushed off to their parents.

Toni turned to Buck. "I thought you didn't want to tell people where it is."

"The sky is beginning to clear up. We may be able to see what the rangers are doing with the mother bear from up there."

"You can't see that from where the sheep horn is."

"Not from there, but remember when we skirted around to the front of the mountain and could see the road below us?"

"Yeah, but I don't think—"

Declan and Anna returned, interrupting Toni.

"Dad says Liam's too tired for another hike and Mom wants to look around in the center," Declan said.

"Sorry," Anna added. They said good-bye just as K'eyush came over, holding a box of compasses and maps.

"I'll go put these away," K'eyush said, "and then escort

you to a bus."

"We're heading for a bus too." Romana had come up behind them. "They can come with us."

"Will that be okay with you two?" K'eyush asked.

"Sure," Buck said.

"Thank you," K'eyush said to Romana, then she turned back to Buck and Toni. "It's been nice meeting you. I'll make sure I watch your show."

Buck and Toni followed the Rails onto a bus. This time the driver was a woman. She whispered to Buck and Toni, "The best views going back will be on the right."

Buck slid into the first vacant right-side seat he saw. Toni sat beside him. Romana found a seat three seats behind them, but Gerald had stopped to talk with the bus driver. As he headed back toward Romana, he stopped beside Buck and Toni.

"I asked the bus driver to let us off at the bottom of Stony Dome," Gerald said. "Why don't you guys come hiking with us? You could show us where that sheep horn is."

"Sure!" Buck said without any hesitation. Toni started to say something, but the bus driver's voice through the intercom cut her off.

"Be seated quickly, please," she said. "We're ready to go." Gerald hurried to his seat.

"I don't think we should go without our dads' permission," Toni told Buck. "They'll be really angry if we do."

"It will be okay," Buck said. "It's not like we're going with strangers. And I know we'll be able to see what's going on from up high."

"What if the bus driver won't let us off?"

"We got on the bus with the Rails, so she probably thinks we belong to them. She'll let us all off together. So, are you in?"

"I guess so, but I still don't think it's a good idea."

A few miles down the road, just before going up the hairpin turns, the bus pulled to a stop and the four got off.

"Good luck, intrepid hikers!" the driver said. She gave them a salute before she closed the door and continued down the road.

As Romana snapped a fanny pack around her waist, Gerald opened a side pocket on his backpack and pulled out a canister of bear spray. Then Buck led the way across the valley, heading toward the knuckle ridge.

This time they saw no caribou. Nor did they see any other animals as they hiked up the mountain. Leading the way, Buck went around the rock pile and had just gone over the rise when he stopped short. In the middle of the flat below him, two short parallel lines smashed down the tundra.

"What an unusual feature," Gerald said. "Who would expect such a big flat piece of land way up here in these mountains?"

"Where's the sheep horn? Is it down there?" Romana asked.

"No, it's on the side of that mountain over there," Buck said, pointing to the left. "Go on down. I have to tie my shoe."

Romana and Gerald started down, angling toward the mountain on the left. Toni started to go too, but Buck put his hand on her shoulder to stop her.

"Did you see those lines?" Buck whispered when the Rails were out of earshot.

"Yeah, where do you think they came from?"

"I don't know. Straight parallel lines don't happen in nature."

Buck took a couple of pictures, and they started down the hill.

"You know what else is weird?" he said.

"What?"

"When you looked down there just now, what was the first thing that caught your eye?"

"The lines."

"Right," Buck said. "Gerald didn't mention the lines at all. All he said was it was flat."

"Yeah, but we saw it without those lines yesterday, so to us they really stand out. But he might think they've been there all along, just part of the tundra."

"Yeah, I guess you're right."

Romana and Gerald had slowed their pace as they started to climb the other mountain. Buck and Toni easily caught up with them. Buck took up the lead, skirting the side of the mountain as they had done with Craig. As soon as the rockslide was in sight, Gerald rushed ahead, almost running.

"Is this it? Is it the right rockslide?" It was only a few seconds before Gerald called back again. "Romana, come over here and look at this. It's fabulous! A perfect specimen!"

Romana hurried over. Gerald took off his backpack, leaned down, and picked up the horn. Then he did the same thing Buck had done the day before. He held it to his head.

"Get the camera out," Gerald said. After taking several pictures, Gerald looked at his watch.

"We'd better get going," he said. "We have a bus to catch."

"We'll keep skirting this mountain and then drop back down to the valley so we won't have to backtrack," Buck said. He picked up the sheep horn and put it back in the rockslide.

Gerald reached down and picked up his backpack, but instead of swinging it up onto his shoulders, he put it back down onto the ground.

"You guys go on ahead. I have to make a nature call," Gerald said. "I'll catch up with you."

"Just a second," Romana said. She took off her fleece

and handed it to Gerald. "Put this in your backpack. I'm getting hot."

"That's why I carry this big old thing around," Gerald said teasingly as he stuffed the red fleece inside. "I have to carry all the stuff Romana just has to bring."

"Well, you never know what you might need," Romana said in defense as she, Buck, and Toni walked away. When they were out of Gerald's sight, Romana suggested they stop and wait. "We don't want to get too far away from him. It's safer to stay in a group."

"Yeah, and he's got the bear spray," Toni added.

When Gerald caught up, they continued skirting the mountain until they reached where the valley spread out beneath them and the road stretched out beyond that. Buck lifted his binoculars. He followed the road as far as he could, hoping to see the ranger trucks parked near the grizzly sow.

"What do you see?" Toni asked.

"Nothing. The road curves behind a hill. You can't see a thing," Buck said as he let the binoculars hang from his neck.

The rest of the way down the mountain and back to the road was uneventful. Buck followed Craig's way down almost exactly, choosing specific draws and slopes and avoiding others.

"It's amazing how I can recognize rocks and even bushes we passed yesterday," he told Toni.

At the road, Gerald took off his bear spray and stowed it in a pocket in his backpack. He stretched his back and rubbed his shoulders as they waited for a green bus to take them back to Tek. They didn't wait long, though. Soon a bus pulled over, and its doors opened.

Buck and Toni kept their eyes peeled as they drove past where the rangers had been parked. They were surprised there were no trucks, no cones, no signs, and, looking as hard as they could, no bears. Not even the grizzly sow. Disappointed, they sat back as the bus continued its long journey to Tek.

TAKE 12:

"A GRIZZLY'S EYESIGHT IS AS GOOD AS A HUMAN'S-AND UNLIKE SOME ANIMALS, IT CAN SEE IN COLOR."

Buck and Toni didn't get back to the campground until almost suppertime. When they walked into the campsite, Dad stuck his head out the door.

"Did you kids have fun at the compass class?" he asked.

"Yeah, it was great," Buck said as they headed toward the Green Beast. "And guess what. The bear cubs are missing! The rangers are trying to figure out where they are."

"I'm sure they will," Dad said dismissively. "But come on in here. We can't wait to show you what we got done today. You're going to love it."

Buck and Toni climbed into the Green Beast. The four of them squished around the table where Shoop's laptop sat. Shoop ceremoniously pushed play.

"This is so cool!" Buck said as the video started. "There I am sneaking through the tundra! It looks just like a real TV show!"

"It will be, dude," Shoop said, chuckling.

Soon a grizzly with two cubs could be seen in the distance, feasting on blueberries. With the bears behind him, Buck also started eating blueberries. At one point, the camera zoomed in on the darker cub until it nearly filled the screen. The sow stood up on her hind legs and roared. The dark cub raced back to its mother. She spanked it and they returned to eating blueberries. At the same time, Buck's voice could be heard saying, *We're using a powerful zoom lens to see the bears up close. No one should ever approach a bear. Remember, we're not on top of the food chain here in Denali!* At that, the video cut over to the scene showing the grizzly taking down the caribou.

"Wow!" Buck said. He could tell why Dad and Shoop were so excited. "That's unbelievable! It's all out of order, but it doesn't look like it."

"If I hadn't seen it with my own eyes," Toni said, "I would have thought it really happened just this way."

"Your dad's the best, Toni," Dad said. "That's why he's called One-Shot Shoop!"

"Nah, just your basic cutting and pasting," Shoop said, but he was smiling.

They continued watching, seeing Craig load the tranquilizer into the rifle, Buck looking at the sleeping grizzly's paws, and the helicopter taking the darted bear away. They saw Buck standing among the herd of caribou, and later balancing across the knife-edge. An Arctic ground squirrel fiercely lectured him as he crawled into the bear's den, and an eagle lifted off, flying over his head, the top of Denali in the distance, floating above the clouds. The video ended with the moose shot.

"It's only a little more than half done," Dad said. "We still need to add about twenty minutes' worth into the middle, but with the beginning and ending done, the hardest parts are behind us. I think it will be a hit!"

"Play back the moose part again," Buck said. Shoop

fast-forwarded the video until Buck stood, a grazing bull moose on the hill behind him. The moose lifted its head and its antlers glowed. Then, in one of the rays that radiated from its antlers, golden words started appearing as if someone were actually writing with a ray of light. *The Wild World* flowed from one antler point, and from another came the words *of Buck Bray!* Buck watched intently as the moose lifted its head, and his own voice overlay could be heard, saying, *"Join us next week for another episode of The Wild World of Buck Bray."*

"That's awesome how the writing comes out of the moose's antlers," Buck said, "just as I say the words. It was almost like I was reading the rays of light."

"It was a little tricky," Shoop stated. "I had to edit the green bus out of the background. Remember how one came around the bend just after the moose trotted away? I thought I had missed it when filming, but you could see it behind the moose."

"That was a lucky shot all the way around," Toni added. "Remember? The audio was messed up by that helicopter too. But you did a great job syncing Buck's voice in, Shoop."

"Thanks," Shoop said, then looked at his watch. "No wonder I'm starved. I can't get used to the time around here. You'd think it's early afternoon by the looks of that sun."

"I'll get the grill started," Dad stated. "Buck, heat up some beans."

Dad grabbed a package of pork chops from the refrigerator. Shoop turned off the computer and followed Dad outside. Toni headed for the door too, but Buck stopped her.

"We need to look at that moose shot again," he whispered.

"Why?"

"I saw something else."

"Are you sure? I didn't see anything. What was it?"

"I don't know. I didn't get a good look, but there's definitely something there that isn't supposed to be."

"Okay," Toni said. She looked out the window. Shoop and Dad were both standing by a small gas grill they had placed on the picnic table. "But we have to be quick. Shoop would kill me if he caught me messing with his laptop."

Toni opened the laptop but hesitated.

"They'll hear it when I start it up," she said.

Buck thought for a moment and then opened a drawer, pulled out a hammer and nails and stuck his head out the door.

"Hey, Dad. Can I hang the 'Bear Danger' sign on my door?"

"Sure," Dad answered.

Buck made a racket pounding the sign to the door as Toni started the computer and brought up the program. She pushed mute as Buck joined her, and fast-forwarded the video to the moose shot.

"Stop. Right there," Buck said.

Toni pushed another key, and the image froze. Buck bent forward to look more closely at the screen.

"Now zoom in on this area over here."

Buck pointed to some alders that were quite a ways from where the moose stood. As Toni zoomed in, the image became pixelated. They couldn't tell what it was, but the color was unmistakable.

"Rek's red backpack!" Buck said. His eyes met Toni's for

just a second before they both turned back to the screen.

"And look at that!" Toni said. She pointed to a hint of a black shape beside the tiny bit of red. Buck looked. It was a squarelike shape. A shape that doesn't usually appear in nature.

"It looks like Rek's black case!" he said.

"Are you sure?" Toni said, shutting down the computer. "I really couldn't tell what either the red or black things were."

"I don't know, but I'm certain they have something to do with the missing cubs," Buck said as he opened a can of beans.

"Shouldn't we show this to Shoop and your dad?" Toni said.

"No, you heard Dad. He hardly paid any attention when I told him the cubs were missing. And Shoop would just edit that stuff out of the shot and we'd lose the evidence. What we need to do is find out what's in that case."

"It might not have even been his case. It could have been something else," Toni argued. "Just because Rek's a jerk doesn't mean he has anything to do with the cubs."

"That's why we have to see what's in it," Buck said. "Whatever's inside that case could prove he's involved somehow."

"I guess so," Toni said just as Dad announced the pork chops were ready.

Dad and Shoop ate slowly, talking business almost nonstop, but Buck and Toni rushed through dinner.

"We're going for a walk," Buck announced. "We'll stay in the campground."

"You were gone all day. Aren't you guys worn-out yet?" Dad asked.

"Some people camping here were in our compass class today, and Toni promised she'd show them her sketchbook," Buck said quickly.

"Well, okay. But don't stay too long and don't leave the campground."

"We'll be back before dark," Buck said, laughing, then turned to Toni. "I've been dying to say that for two weeks!"

Toni grabbed her backpack. "Where are we going?" she asked as they headed over to the first loop.

"To Rek's campsite," Buck answered.

"You don't even know if Rek's case is still there," Toni said. "And if it is, how are you going to see what's in it without getting caught?"

"You can cause a distraction. I'll climb into the car real quick, open it up, and take a look."

"What if the door's locked? Or the case isn't in the car anymore? Or what if Rek catches you? What are you going to do then?"

"I don't know. We'll just see when we get there, okay?"

They were almost to Site 13. Stopping behind a spruce tree at the edge of Site 12, they peered into the next campsite. They could see a black car, but it blocked their view of the tent. They crept deeper into the trees that separated the two campsites until they could see better. A green tent was set up beside the picnic table.

"Are we at the right spot?" Buck whispered. "I could have sworn he had a blue tent."

"He did," Toni said.

"Grrrr-roar," a deep growl thundered out right behind them. Buck nearly jumped out of his skin, and Toni gasped as they both spun around. Gerald stood there, laughing.

"You two sure are jumpy," he said. "Thought it was a bear, didn't you?"

Romana was also laughing, from the doorway of an RV parked in Site 12.

"No, you just startled us," Buck said. He quickly made up an excuse for being in the trees. "We thought we saw a moose in that campsite, but it ended up being just a shadow."

"Yeah," Toni said. "We were actually looking for you guys. I want to show you my sketchbook." Toni pulled her sketchbook from her backpack.

"Wonderful. Come on in," Romana said. "We can see better inside."

Toni walked toward the RV. Gerald followed, but Buck hesitated. *I need to get a better look at Rek's campsite,* he thought.

"I'll be just a second," he called out. "Need to hit the outhouse first."

"You can use our RV's john," Gerald said.

"That's okay," Buck said. "I like outhouses."

"Didn't I tell you, Romana?" Gerald said as he headed

for the RV. "For some strange reason, kids just seem to have a fascination with outhouses. They're always going in and out, in and out."

"Just the boys," Toni said. "I prefer the one in our RV."

Buck just shrugged and headed for the road. As soon as he heard the RV door close, he turned back around. This time, instead of going in between campsites, he walked right to the front of Site 13 and looked down the drive. In it was a black car. A green tent. A picnic table. A bike leaned against a spruce by the path that led to the river, and a boy with a hoodie sweatshirt stood near the fire ring, holding a handful of kindling. A small trickle of smoke came up from the fire ring. The boy looked up at Buck.

"Hi," he said. "What's up?"

"Nothing much," Buck said. "I saw you at the airport the other day. Just thought I'd say hi. When did you get here?"

"My mom and I got here just before noon today and couldn't believe this site was open. It's the best site in loop one. There's a better spot in loop two, but it was taken. Some weird-looking green camper is there. Have you seen it?"

"Yeah, it's beastly," Buck said, smiling to himself. "Did you happen to see the guy who was camping here before you?"

"Was his name Rek Malkum?" the boy answered.

"Yeah! Do you know him?"

"No, he left his registration tag on the post. I never saw him."

"Too bad," Buck said. "He had a really cool bear claw on his backpack."

"Wow," the boy said. "I wish I had seen that!"

"Well, I have to go," Buck said. "Maybe I'll see you around."

"Okay, see ya," the boy said, and returned to putting sticks on the fire.

Buck went back to the Rails' RV, knocked on the door, and walked in. It was much bigger than the Green Beast. To the right was a living area. The driver's and passenger's seats swiveled around to make lounge chairs, and there was even a couch. Toni sat on it between Romana and Gerald, her sketchbook open on her lap, a pencil in her hand. Buck glanced at what she was drawing. The Dall sheep horn. Then he sat down in one of the lounge chairs and looked across the living area toward the kitchen.

"Wow! You guys have a TV?" he said. Built into the wall was a small set.

"Gerald can't do without watching the news every day," Romana said.

"News?" Buck asked. "How can you get news here?"

"Come here. I'll show you," Gerald said, getting up and heading toward a door beyond the kitchen. "You're going to love this."

"I'm not sure everything is put away in there, Gerald," Romana said.

"Yes, it is. I put everything away while you were cooking supper."

"My mom is like that too," Toni said without even looking up. "Doesn't want one little thing out of place. Shoop drives her crazy."

Romana smiled and said, "I guess I'm just a neat freak."

Buck followed Gerald through the door. A bed sat in the middle of the room, with space to walk on either side. On the back wall, narrow closet doors stood on each side of the bed. The room was neat as a pin. The only thing out of place was Gerald's backpack. It sat on the bed, its top flap lying open across a quilt. Something was sticking out of the top. Over Gerald's shoulder, Buck couldn't see what it was. Just a little point of something. Something brown. Gerald nonchalantly reached over and flipped the flap of the backpack closed. Then he walked over to a closet, opened the door, and shoved some clothes aside.

"See that thing?" he said, pointing to a little crank on the ceiling. "Turn that, and a satellite dish pops up on the top of the RV. We can get TV, Internet, cell phone, everything."

"Cool!" Buck said.

Toni didn't even look up as they came back into the kitchen. "Shoop's been telling your dad he needs to update the Green Beast. He says your dad is the biggest procrastinator about technology he's ever seen."

"It's true. Dad doesn't even have an electric coffee-maker," Buck explained to the Rails. "He makes it in a pot on the stove."

"Just bring him over here," Romana said. "We'll get

him convinced."

"You don't know my dad. He wouldn't even let me bring DVDs to watch on his laptop. You'd think being a TV personality, he'd want to watch stuff, but he says it's distracting when he's on a shoot."

Gerald sat down again, but Buck headed for the door.

"We'd better get going, Toni," he said. "Maybe we'll see you guys tomorrow."

"I doubt it," Gerald said. "We're leaving tomorrow morning."

"It was great hiking with you two," Romana said. "We can't wait to see your show."

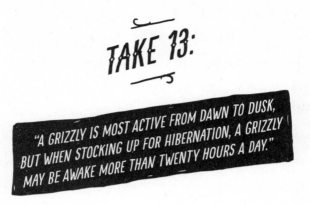

TAKE 13:

"A GRIZZLY IS MOST ACTIVE FROM DAWN TO DUSK, BUT WHEN STOCKING UP FOR HIBERNATION, A GRIZZLY MAY BE AWAKE MORE THAN TWENTY HOURS A DAY."

"Did you see inside the case?" Toni asked as soon as the RV door closed.

"No, Rek left. Did you notice that kid at the airport with the hoodie? He and his mom are camping there now. He said they got there this afternoon. But I'm certain Rek has something to do with the missing cubs," Buck said as they walked up the campground road. "I just can't figure it all out. The bears were there after the moose shot on Tuesday. And we now know Rek was hiding nearby when we shot the moose."

"The bears were missing Wednesday morning," Toni added, "and remember, on the bus Monday? It looked like Rek was taking GPS coordinates of every animal, including the sow and cubs."

"Wait a second. We have to get organized," Buck said. "Give me your sketchbook and a pencil." Buck sat down at a table in a vacant campsite. "It's just like with a shoot. We have all these different episodes recorded all out of order, but then we have to put them together so they'll make sense."

Buck turned to a new page in the sketchbook and wrote *Missing Grizzly Cubs* at the top. The two of them started naming off all the important clues they could think of, and Buck wrote them down in the correct order.

1. SUN—Saw man with red backpack and black case at airport. His name is Rek Malkum and he camped at Site 13.

2. MON—Saw cubs with the sow. Rek took GPS readings of bears' location.

3. TUES—Rek was hiding in the bushes during the

moose shot. Saw his red backpack and black case in the
video. Saw cubs with sow after the moose shot.
4. WED—Cubs gone in morning before first bus got there.
New campers moved into Site 13 before noon so Rek left
Tek before noon.

Buck finished writing and read it out loud.

"There's something missing," Toni said.

"Yeah, the most important part," Buck said. "How he did it."

"And why," Toni added.

"Why is easy. For money," Buck said. "Some rich guy will pay a lot of money to have his own personal bear cubs."

"But that's illegal."

"Yeah, that's why we have to catch Rek."

"I think we should tell our dads."

"They'd just say we're imagining things. But if we can figure out how he did it, then they'd believe us."

As they walked back through loop one and headed toward loop two, they brainstormed more.

"He couldn't just grab two bear cubs," Toni said. "The sow would kill him."

"That's another easy one. Rek could have tranquilized the sow and the cubs."

"But how would he have gotten them out of there?" Toni asked. "He can't just walk onto a green bus carrying two bear cubs."

Buck stopped. "I think I know what he did. He tranquilized them. Then came back here, packed up his camp, drove back, and put them in his car. But he'd have to have time. Do you remember what time it was when we shot the moose scene?"

"I don't know," Toni answered, "but we got back to Tek before eight, so it had to be around five thirty. Why?"

"I think I've got it! Come on! We have to find out what time the last bus leaves."

They ran to the main road and over to the bus stop. Tacked to the wall on the inside of the pavilion was a schedule. Buck followed his finger down a column.

"You were close. The bus we saw just after the moose shot left Eielson at five thirty. It takes about fifteen minutes to get where we shot the moose. That must have been the bus Shoop edited out of the moose scene. So it went past us at about five forty-five. We left shortly afterward and saw the sow and cubs. So they were still there at about five fifty-five or so."

Buck quickly jotted the times down in Toni's sketchbook. Then he turned back to the schedule, tracked another column, and scribbled down more times, explaining as he wrote.

"There was only one more bus after the five-thirty one. It left Eielson at six thirty. So it went past Stony Dome at about six forty-five and was back here at Tek about eight fifty."

"So?" Toni said.

"Don't you see? It was the last bus. Rek was still hiding out there when we left, so he had to get on that six-thirty bus, and it got to Tek at eight fifty."

"I still don't see what difference that makes."

"It's all about timing. Rek was here at almost nine. It would take him about two and a half hours to get from Tek back to the tranquilized bears and then another two and a half hours back to Tek. That's five hours." Buck looked at the schedule again. "Add another forty-five minutes to get to the checkpoint and another thirty to the park entrance. That's six hours and fifteen minutes."

Buck looked at the schedule one last time. "The first bus coming into the park in the morning gets to Tek at seven twenty-five, and it would take two and a half hours before it would get to the bears. That's about ten o'clock. So . . ." Buck started counting backward on his fingers, but Toni spoke up before he could finish.

"I get it! He'd have to leave Tek by three forty-five in the morning on Wednesday in order to have time to get the bears and get out of the park before Jerry came along in the first bus and found the cubs gone!"

"Except he'd have to have time to get the bears into the car, too," Buck said, "so if he left Tek by two forty-five, that would give him an hour to mess with the cubs."

"We've done it! We've figured it out!" Toni was so excited, she was jumping up and down. Buck was already running from the bus stop.

"Come on!" he yelled back. "Let's go ask Romana and

Gerald what time Rek left Tek! They would surely hear someone starting a car in the middle of the night. That would prove our theory."

When they got to the Rails' campsite, the blinds had been shut and the RV was dark. Buck listened but couldn't hear a TV playing.

"They must have gone to bed," Toni said.

"Yeah, we'll have to get over here to ask them before they leave tomorrow morning," Buck said. He opened the sketchbook and crossed out clue number four and wrote two new clues.

4. TUES/WED—Rek left Tek between 9:00 Tues. night and 2:45 Wed. morning to get cubs and get totally out of the park before cubs were found missing.

5. WED—Cubs gone in morning before first bus got there. New camper moved into Site 13 before noon.

"He'd probably leave after sunset so no one would see him," Toni said after reading what Buck wrote. Buck crossed off *9:00*, wrote in *10:24*, and handed the sketchbook back to Toni.

Satisfied, they headed back to loop two. Soon they could see Shoop through the window, sitting at the table in his RV and working on his laptop.

"Should we tell our dads now?" Toni said.

"We don't want to accuse someone without proof," Buck said. "We'll know as soon as we talk with the Rails in the morning. Then we'll tell our dads. They wouldn't do anything tonight anyway."

"Okay, see you in the morning," Toni said, and headed toward her RV.

Dad was sitting outside by a small campfire when Buck got back to the Green Beast.

"The show is going to be awesome!" Buck said, pulling up a chair and trying to act like nothing else was on his mind.

"I think so too. To be honest, I had my doubts about whether this whole thing would work. I was worried about how responsible you'd be. But I'm not worried anymore." Dad reached over and patted Buck on the shoulder. "You're doing a great job, and I'm really proud of you."

"Thanks," Buck said.

"So, tell me about your day. How was the compass class?"

Buck told his dad about K'eyush and talked excitedly about the student conservation program and how he would like to be involved with something like that when he was older. But as they watched the fire burn to embers, Buck kept quiet about his theory on how the cubs were taken. He also decided not to ruin the moment by telling his dad about their hike with the Rails.

TAKE 14:

"ALTHOUGH GRIZZLIES HEAR, SEE, AND SMELL WELL, THEY OFTEN DON'T PAY ANY ATTENTION TO WHAT'S GOING ON AROUND THEM AND CAN BLUNDER INTO AN UNSUSPECTING HUMAN."

THURSDAY, AUGUST 15

It rained all night. Usually the sound of the rain on the roof of the Green Beast put Buck right to sleep, but tonight several things nagged at his mind.

I should have told Dad we hiked with the Rails, Buck thought. *But I will. As soon as I can prove my theory about Rek. Maybe he won't be so upset if he knows how interested I am in what happened to those cubs.*

As he lay there thinking, another thing came to his mind. *Why didn't the Rails ever say they were camped next to Rek? I know they got a good look at him on the bus. But there's probably a simple explanation.* He lay there a while longer, listening to the rain. Suddenly it dawned on him. *That's it! The Rails are on the buses every day, and when they get back, they go inside. Gerald has to watch the news. They've probably never noticed who's camped next to them. I don't have a clue who's camped beside us.*

Buck tossed and turned. *It still seems like I'm missing something else though,* he thought until he finally drifted off to sleep.

In the morning, as soon as they finished breakfast, Buck and Toni hurried to the first loop. The rain had cleared out, and the sky was bright blue. When they got to the Rails' campsite, Gerald was pulling out walking sticks from one of the outdoor compartments on the RV. Romana was coming out the door, snapping a fanny pack that held two bottles of water around her waist.

"Good morning," Romana called out cheerfully.

"I thought you guys were leaving," Buck said.

"We are, but checkout isn't until eleven," Romana said. "We're going to explore the riverbed this morning before we leave."

"What brings you two here so early?" Gerald asked.

"We have a question," Buck said. "Do you know when the man in Site Thirteen left?"

"There's a woman and her son in that campsite. I met the woman this morning," Romana stated. "She's very nice."

"No, we mean the person there before them," Toni said. "It was a man named Rek."

"Oh, we never met him," Romana stated. "He left Tuesday morning."

Buck and Toni looked at each other, surprised. "Tuesday morning? Are you sure it wasn't yesterday morning?"

"No, it was first thing Tuesday," Gerald said. "We were surprised nobody took that site until yesterday. Why?"

Buck didn't get a chance to answer because suddenly a low-flying helicopter buzzed past. It circled around, came back, and hovered right above them. Craig was looking out the window. He waved and then pointed his finger several times back toward the second loop.

"Come on, Toni!" Buck yelled over the noise of the spinning blades. "Craig's in there, and I think he wants us to get back to the Green Beast."

Campers were rushing out from RVs, tents, and trailers as Buck and Toni ran from the first loop to the second. Everyone was headed toward the river. When Buck and Toni reached the Green Beast, Dad and Shoop were not in sight. The two kids didn't even slow down. They ran right down the path to the river. Dad and Shoop were there, and so was Craig. The helicopter sat out in the middle of the riverbed.

"Let's go back to the Green Beast," Craig said. "We've stirred up quite a bit of commotion, and I want to talk in private."

They had to push past a flow of people rushing through their campsite and down the path to take pictures of the helicopter, but soon the five of them were crammed into the Green Beast. Craig and Toni sat on one of the benches at the table; Dad and Buck sat across from them. Shoop stood beside them, his laptop on the table.

"I don't know if you've heard, but the two cubs are missing . . . ," Craig started.

"Buck told us yesterday," Dad said. "Do you know what happened to them?"

"No, not yet. That's why I came," Craig said. "For two reasons. You guys are observant. Have you noticed anything unusual or seen anything strange in your recordings?"

"No," Dad said, but Buck glanced over at Toni and took a deep breath.

"Toni and I have," he said. "When we shot the moose, someone was out on the tundra."

"We could see a red spot and black shape in the moose shot," Toni added.

"You didn't tell us," Dad said, looking hard at Buck.

Buck started, "We were going to but—"

Dad interrupted. "Shoop, let's take a look."

"I'll show you," Toni said. She pulled Shoop's laptop over in front of her, brought up the last part of the show, and zoomed in. She pointed out the red spot to Craig. Dad and Shoop also took a look.

"I don't know," Shoop said. "It's just a little red spot. It doesn't look like a person."

"We think it's a red backpack," Buck said. Then he pointed to the black shape. "And we think that's the corner of a black case that belongs to Rek."

"Who's Rek?" Craig asked. Buck told them everything he knew about Rek and his and Toni's suspicions. "But it couldn't be him. The Rails told us he left Tek on Tuesday morning."

"Who are the Rails?" Dad asked.

"Romana and Gerald," Toni said. "An older couple we met Monday on the bus. She's the one who bandaged my finger."

"They're camping at Site Twelve," Buck said. "And Rek was camped next to them in Site Thirteen."

"The Rails were in our compass class, too," Toni added. "And—" She started to say more, but Craig interrupted.

"K'eyush told me you knew some people in the class," Craig said. This time he was looking hard at Buck. "She was a little worried when the driver told her you got off the bus to go hiking with a couple of them."

"You what?" Dad exploded.

"The Rails wanted to see the sheep horn," Buck said, his eyes not meeting Dad's or Craig's. "And we thought maybe we could see what was going on with the bears from up there."

"And you never told me?" Dad yelled.

"I'm sorry," Buck said quietly.

"Sorry doesn't cut it," Dad said.

"Toni, you were in on this too," Shoop said.

"I know. I'm sorry. We should have told you."

"It wasn't her fault," Buck said. "I talked her into it."

"You need to sort that all out later," Craig said. "There's another reason I came here."

"What?" Dad asked.

"We still haven't found the cubs. I think the kids are right. Probably somebody has taken them, and we're already looking into that. The kids' information will be of help. But we want to do an aerial search, too, just in case. See if we can find either the cubs or perhaps a cache if another bear has killed them. And that's where you guys come in."

"Us?" Shoop asked. "How?"

"Well, I was thinking this could be a win-win situation for both of us," Craig said. "You might be able to use some aerial shots in your show. It's a clear morning; we could even zip around Denali after we're done. There's not a cloud on it. That will help you out. And maybe something that shows up in your footage, like that red backpack and black case, will give us some clues, too. You're really good with that camera, Shoop."

Shoop had been standing beside the table, but now he backed up all the way to the bathroom door, shaking his head frantically.

"No way," Shoop said. "Absolutely no way."

"I'm sorry," Craig said. "I forgot you're afraid of heights."

"Shoop, I can go," Toni said quietly. "I know how to run the camera."

Shoop looked at his daughter and gave her a smile. "Thanks. You're a good kid," he said, then turned to Craig. "It's okay with me if it's okay with you."

"That's fine," Craig said to Shoop, then looked at Dad. "How long will it take you to get ready?"

"Five minutes," Dad said.

"Okay," Craig said to Dad. "I'll tell the pilot you and Toni will be joining us."

"What about me?" Buck asked.

"I can only take two extra people," Craig said.

"Oh man, that's not fair," Buck complained.

"Buck has to go," Toni stated. "He has to be in the shots."

Buck looked at Dad. He still looked angry. "Can't I go? Please?"

"If Toni wasn't right, there's no way I'd let you go. Not after you went hiking when you were supposed to stay on the bus. And then you purposely kept it a secret from me. How do I know I can trust you now?"

Buck looked Dad in the eyes. "I messed up, but it won't happen again."

"Well, we'll discuss that tonight," Dad said. "Now, do you promise you'll do exactly as Craig says? No extra side trips?"

"We promise," Buck and Toni said together.

"Okay, I'll meet you at the chopper," Craig said.

As Dad and Shoop were getting the camera equipment ready, Buck turned to Toni.

"Thanks," he said.

"No problem," Toni replied. "After all, you made sure I

got to go into the bear den."

It seemed like most of the people camping at Tek were down on the riverbed. Now they took pictures of Buck in his official shirt and Toni with a camera bag as they walked across gravel bars to the helicopter. The chopper's blades sat motionless and silent. Craig stood beside it, waiting for them.

"This helicopter is bigger than the one that came to the caribou kill," Buck said.

"That was a park helicopter. Sometimes, if ours are really busy, we hire out a private chopper and pilot," Craig said as he opened the door. "This is the first time I've flown with this guy."

Buck climbed in first. There was a large panel of gauges, dials, buttons, and switches in the front of the cockpit. More buttons and switches were on the ceiling. The pilot sat on the right, a control stick between his legs. At his feet were two pedals. He wasn't wearing a ranger uniform. He had on a flannel shirt, wraparound sunglasses, and over his ball cap was a headset with earphones and a mic that curved to his mouth. There was a similar headset on the empty seat beside the pilot, and two more hanging on the wall behind the two backseats.

Buck scrambled across the console between the two backseats, sat down behind the pilot, and buckled his seat belt. Toni climbed in, put her backpack under her seat, and reached back for the camera bag Craig was holding up to her. As Craig closed the back door, the pilot started pushing buttons and switches. The motor started to whine, and the chopper vibrated as the blades began to turn.

Craig opened the front door and climbed in. The blades were going faster and faster now, and the noise was getting louder and more high-pitched. The spinning blades made the nearby willow branches wave frantically. Craig picked up a headset, turned around, and yelled back to Buck and Toni.

"Put those headsets on and we'll all be able to hear each other!"

Buck reached for the headsets and handed one to Toni. Instantly the ear-piercing noise was muffled, and they could hear Craig clearly.

"I want you two to keep your seat belts on even when

recording. No getting out of your seats. Is that clear?"

Buck and Toni both answered yes. Craig continued, "This is our pilot, Bernie." They heard Bernie say hi through the headphones but, busy with the controls, he didn't turn around.

"Remember," Craig continued, "if you see anything unusual, tell us so we can go in for a closer look. We're looking for the cubs, of course, but also for male bears, food caches, or anything that looks unusual."

The helicopter slowly lifted as Shoop videoed from below. Then, in one fluid motion, the chopper's nose dropped and the craft swung around. Gaining speed, it followed the riverbed upstream.

"Craig," Buck said through the mic, "those are the Rails down there. Romana's the one with the red fleece on."

The Rails looked up from the riverbed as the chopper headed toward the Teklanika River Bridge. At the bridge, it turned right and followed the road. Toni took her sketchbook from her backpack and handed it to Buck.

"Don't forget," Toni's voice came through the headset. "It's too noisy to have a mic on in here. So write down everything you would say if you're in a shot."

"I know," Buck said. "Shoop said we can lip-sync my voice in later." He slid the sketchbook into the pocket on the back of Bernie's seat and turned to look out the window. Soon they were approaching where the bears were last seen. But the chopper didn't turn to fly over the area. Instead it turned north.

"Maybe we should take a look toward the south," Craig said to Bernie. "Go up that ravine all the way to the cliffs."

"Air traffic control told me someone else will be covering the south side of the road," Bernie answered. "I'm supposed to check out the area downstream."

The helicopter continued following the river valley downstream. Sometimes Craig told Bernie to go in low, checking out willow and alder thickets. Other times they went higher so Craig could scan the spruce forests with binoculars. But other than Alaskan landscapes, they saw nothing.

"Okay," Craig finally said to Bernie. "I guess we've done all we can. Let's do a little flight-seeing before taking the kids back to Tek."

The chopper turned west and went over a ridge, then swept southwest, crossing the road. Soon the road was far behind and they were following a glacier straight toward ice-covered peaks.

"This is phenomenal!" Toni exclaimed. "I've got to shoot this!"

As Toni took out the camera from its case, Buck pulled the sketchbook out of the seat pocket and quickly wrote in it. Toni leaned over the console and read what he wrote, then adjusted the camera.

"Okay, I've got a good angle. Are you ready?"

Buck nodded and looked at the camera.

"Action!" Toni said.

"Look at me fly! Just like an eagle soaring through the air! Mountains all around me, a glacier below me, and look what's ahead! Denali, the Great One!"

Toni kept the camera on Buck as he spoke, and then slowly turned it to face out the front window. The chopper was following a river of ice. The glacier almost looked like a road, curving around the jagged snowcapped mountain peaks that surrounded it. Towering above them at the end of the glacier was the great mountain, white and magnificent, so big that its rugged summits filled the camera lens.

"That's a wrap," Toni called out. She rested the camera in her lap. "Shoop's really going to be excited about that shot."

"He should be," Craig said. "It's incredible up here! I'm glad you guys got to see it. Bernie, drop this thing down low so Toni can get some shots of the glacier up close."

Bernie dropped the helicopter until it was skimming only a few yards above the glacier's surface. From high above it looked like smooth snowfields, but now Buck could see the long sheet of ice was split with deep cracks and crevasses.

"The colors are amazing!" Buck said. In contrast to the dirty grays of the surface ice, the ice in the cracks and crevasses was a brilliant turquoise blue.

"Some of those cracks are hundreds of feet deep," Craig told them.

"Why is it blue?" Toni asked, her camera focused on a deep fissure.

"It's complex, but over time the glacier ice becomes so

compact and dense, it absorbs all the different color rays except blue. The blue color rays escape, so that's what you see."

Craig asked Bernie to fly closer to a jumble of huge ice boulders that had split off from cliffs of ice. Some were bigger than houses and lay like toppled piles of rock. The chopper had barely moved that direction when suddenly, over the headphones, a gritty voice cut in.

"Bravo Alpha Delta four eight niner. This is Alpha Tango Charlie. Over."

"Alpha Tango Charlie. This is Bravo Alpha Delta four eight niner. I read you, over," Bernie said back to the voice.

"Orders to take Craig to Toklat rest area immediately, over," the voice said.

"Affirmative. Roger. Out," Bernie stated. The voice made no more replies.

"Looks like I'm needed at Toklat," Craig said into the headset mic as Bernie swung the helicopter around and accelerated. "Bernie will take you back to Tek after he drops me off."

It wasn't long before the tentlike gift shop and the parking lot were below them. A green bus was just pulling out, and several others were parked side by side. People scattered around the observation area looked up at the chopper as it approached, and one man almost dropped the caribou antlers he held to his head.

The helicopter continued on to an unpaved parking lot that couldn't be seen by the tourists. Some maintenance equipment was parked there, and another ranger stood beside a truck, waiting for Craig. The chopper stopped its forward movement and hovered in midair for a few seconds. After last night's rain the whole parking lot was muddy, and big puddles dotted the area. Waves churned in the puddles as the helicopter hovered above them. Bernie moved the chopper backward slightly so it wouldn't land in a puddle, and soon its skids touched down in the mud. They were landing only long enough for Craig to jump out, so Bernie did not turn off the rotating blades.

"Here, Buck," Craig said, "put my headset in that console." Craig took off his headset and handed it to Buck. Buck opened the console. Inside was a camo jacket.

He pushed the jacket out of the way and gasped. In the bottom of the console sat a red backpack with a curved bear claw attached to the zipper pull.

Buck quickly looked to the front. Bernie was focusing on the dials, paying no attention. Craig had jumped out of the helicopter and was about to close the door. Without hesitating, Buck yelled as loud as he could. Craig looked in at him.

"Yes, Bernie will take you to Tek," Craig yelled back, and then closed the helicopter door. Over the noise of the rotating blades and without a headset, it was clear Craig did not hear him correctly. But everyone else still had on their headsets, and neither Toni nor Bernie had any trouble understanding what Buck had yelled.

"That's not Bernie; it's Rek!"

TAKE 15:

"GRIZZLIES ARE FAST! THEY CAN RUN UP TO THIRTY-FIVE MILES PER HOUR. THAT'S FIFTY-ONE FEET IN ONE SECOND!"

The helicopter rose rapidly above the ranger truck. Toni was looking wild-eyed at Rek. Leaning close to the window, Buck waved both arms frantically, trying to signal to Craig that something was wrong. Craig looked up, smiled, and waved, then turned his back to them to talk with the other ranger.

The helicopter moved quickly away and, as it did, Buck looked back and saw that it had left two parallel lines etched into the mud.

That's what I was forgetting last night! he thought.

"So you think you've got it all figured out, huh, kid?" Rek said as the helicopter gained momentum. Buck didn't answer. "Well, you don't even have a clue."

"We do too," Toni blurted out. "We know you took the bear cubs."

"And you used this helicopter to do it," Buck added. "That's why you didn't fly up the ravine to the cliffs today, isn't it? You didn't want Craig to see where the skids smashed down the tundra on the flat spot above the cliffs."

"Shut up. Both of you," Rek said. Anger was escalating in his voice.

Buck looked at Toni and put his finger to his mouth, then quietly slid the sketchbook from the seat pocket.

It's ok, just keep quiet, he wrote. He held it so Toni could see it but kept the sketchbook low, behind Rek's seat, so it was out of his sight.

Buck turned a page and wrote again.

Rek shaved his beard and mustache, but I should have recognized the sunglasses.

Buck held it up for Toni to read again, then laid the sketchbook on his lap and looked out the window. They were following the road back toward Tek, and soon Buck saw the Teklanika Bridge below and then the two loops of the Tek Campground. But the chopper did not slow down or lose altitude. In fact, it was going higher.

"If you go back and let us out, we promise we won't tell," Buck said.

"You really think I believe that?" Rek sneered.

"You're going to get caught," Toni said. "When Craig gets back to Tek and we're not there—"

Rek interrupted her. "Craig won't be back to the campground for hours. We'll be miles from here by then."

We'll think of something, Buck wrote in the sketchbook, but his heart was beating fiercely as he stared out the window at the park road below him. Without warning, the helicopter turned to the left and headed away from the road.

"Where are you going now?" Buck demanded. "The Denali airport is near the entrance."

Rek ignored Buck. He turned a dial, pushed a button, and started talking again.

"Golf Echo Romeo two five three. This is Bravo Alpha

Delta four eight niner. Over."

Static came through the headphones, and soon another voice.

"Bravo Alpha Delta four eight niner. This is Golf Echo Romeo two five three. I read you, over."

"Change of plans. Move my car from Denali airport to alternate landing location. Over," Rek said.

"Why? Over."

"I have extra baggage. Over."

"How much extra baggage? Over."

"Two. Over."

"What type? Over."

"Immature human. Over."

"Help!" Buck yelled as loud as he could. "He's kidnapping us!"

"Shut up!" Rek snarled. He quickly pushed the button, and the static over the headsets instantly quit.

"He didn't even hear you!" Toni exclaimed.

"Oh, he heard him all right," Rek said. "He just didn't care."

Rek started laughing. Not a funny laugh. A wicked laugh.

"You probably wish you'd kept your mouth shut, Bucko, old boy. I would have had no idea you recognized me. You'd be back at that green camper of yours, spilling the beans, and the rangers would be waiting for me at the Denali airport. So I guess I have you to thank, don't I, Bucko?"

Buck felt his face redden.

He won't get away with it! he wrote.

As he showed it to Toni, he could feel tears well up in his eyes. Toni looked scared too, her face tense. Buck quickly blinked away the tears, and wrote down more, showing Toni the message sentence by sentence.

We'll be all right.

We just have to stay calm.

As Buck looked out the window at the thick spruce forest that covered the mountains below, he quietly took the compass out of his pocket. Then he wrote *Going NE 38°*. He held it up for Toni to see, and she nodded. They kept flying in the same direction until a road became visible in the distance. There were no green buses on it. It was busy with cars and semitrucks. Also in the distance was a small town.

We've left the park, Buck wrote. *We'll probably land soon. I have a plan.* Buck opened to a new page and continued writing.

HELP!!!! Rek Malkum (also called Bernie) kidnapped us. Call Ranger Craig at Denali immediately.

Buck Bray and Toni Shoop

Buck quietly tore the paper out of the sketchbook and showed it to Toni. He slid the note into the seat pocket, but when he looked back out the window, the chopper had gone over the town and was once again flying across the forest. Finally the chopper slowed to a hover above the forest, and Rek's voice came through the headset.

"We'll be landing soon. Toni, get my backpack out of the console."

Toni pulled out the bright red backpack and handed it to Rek. Rek unzipped it and pulled out a canister of bear spray and put it in his lap.

The helicopter regained speed, flying just above the spruces toward the red tin roof of a lodge. Several red-roofed cabins were lined up on either side of it, and a narrow drive wound through the forest in front of the buildings. The drive continued to a clearing with a big square of pavement. A large white circle with a big letter *H* in the middle was painted on the square. Rek's black car was parked near the helicopter pad. The chopper hovered above the circle and landed perfectly within its border.

Rek turned toward the backseats.

"Okay, listen up. If either one of you does anything—yell, run, act at all weird—the other one will get a shot of this," Rek threatened, holding up the bear spray. He flipped the safety off and held his finger on the trigger. "And believe me, if it will hurt a thousand-pound grizzly, it'll hurt you, too. Understand?"

Both Buck and Toni nodded as Rek opened his door, climbed out, and then opened the back door.

"Now get out," Rek commanded. "Bring all your stuff and my jacket, too."

Buck stuffed the sketchbook into Toni's backpack, grabbed Rek's jacket, and climbed out. Toni started to open the door on her side.

"Oh no, you don't, missy," Rek called to her. "You get

out on this side too." Toni scrambled over the console and jumped out beside Buck, the camera bag in her hand. Rek started to shut the door but stopped and looked at the back of his seat. A small corner from a page of paper stuck out of the top of the seat pocket. He reached in, pulled out the piece of paper, and read it.

"Thought you were pretty smart, didn't you?" He angrily crammed the paper into his pocket and then grabbed Buck tightly by the arm.

"Toni, get in front of me, walk normally over to the car, and open the front door," Rek said, still grasping Buck's arm. "Now, see that lever beside the seat? Pull it up."

Toni did as he instructed, and the trunk opened.

"I can't trust you'll stay out of sight in the car, so get back there and climb in," Rek commanded. "Quickly!"

Toni put the camera bag into the trunk and scrambled in.

"Your turn, Bucko." Rek gave Buck a hard shove. Buck hit his head on the edge of the trunk lid as he fell in, landing on what looked like Rek's blue tent. He quickly pulled his feet in just as Rek slammed the lid down. Suddenly it was pitch-black. A few seconds later the car started and they were driving away.

"Do you think he's going to kill us?" Toni asked, her voice cracking between sobs.

Tears were sliding down Buck's cheeks too. He took a deep breath and forced himself to sound calm.

"No," he said, wiping his tears away. "He would have just left us in the wilderness for the grizzlies."

Buck squirmed around. "Lift your head up. We can use the tent as a pillow."

The two lay quietly on their backs. The air was stale, and they heard the whine of the tires on the pavement. At first the car moved slowly, making several turns. Then it sped up, driving over a twisty, curvy road.

"Does your watch light up?" Buck asked.

A faint light suddenly glowed on Toni's wrist. The watch didn't offer much light, but there was enough for her to get a look at Buck.

"You're bleeding," she said.

"I know," Buck said, touching his forehead. He could feel the sticky blood on his fingers. "I hit my head when Rek shoved me. I'll be okay, though." As he talked, he pulled the compass out of his pocket.

"We're heading south. We must be on the highway we took to get to Denali," Buck said. "What time is it?"

"A quarter till one," she stated. "Why?"

"We can guess how far we've gone if we know how long we've been driving," Buck said.

"I wonder if there's a flashlight or something in here," Toni said. "My battery will go dead if the light's on too long."

Buck squirmed around again until he was on his hands and knees, and then he felt around in the dim light. A T-shirt, a rain jacket, and an open box. He rummaged through the box. It contained a couple of cans of soup, a roll of duct tape, and a granola bar. Just one. Buck took out the granola bar and then pushed everything back into a corner as far as possible to give them more room. He then scrambled around until he was lying on his back again.

"Did you find anything?" Toni asked, letting her watch go dark again.

"No flashlight, but there's a granola bar. We can share it."

Buck broke the granola bar and gave half to Toni.

"I keep thinking I have it all figured out, but then something messes it up," Buck said between bites. "On Monday, Rek took GPS readings so he could locate the cubs by air. Once he knew where the cubs were, he didn't need to stay at Tek, so he left Tuesday morning. But this is where it messes up. I know he flew in to get those cubs, and at some point he landed on the flat."

"So how's that messed up?" Toni asked. "Rek saw us shooting the moose, parked the helicopter on the flat until we were gone, and then flew down and got the cubs."

"That won't work," Buck said. "Don't you see? He can't be in two places at once."

Toni thought for a moment. "You're right. He can't be hiding in the bushes and flying a helicopter at the same time. We're still missing something."

TAKE 16:

"A GRIZZLY BEAR'S BEHAVIOR IS USUALLY MORE PREDICTABLE THAN A HUMAN'S. THEY ARE MAINLY CONCERNED WITH PROTECTING THEIR YOUNG, THEIR FOOD, AND THEIR PERSONAL SPACE."

Buck and Toni had gone through all the possibilities they could think of and were now silent. They lay there, each with their own thoughts, as the car continued down the road. Finally the car started slowing down.

"Are you awake?" Buck lightly shook Toni.

"Yeah, I'm awake."

"Remember the town we saw with all the gift shops and lodges? I think we're going through it now."

"Maybe we're going back to the park!" Toni said, her voice sounding hopeful. "If we yell when we get there, maybe someone will hear us."

But the car never turned and before long, it was gaining speed again.

"We've gone past the park entrance, haven't we?" Toni said.

"I think so," Buck said. He let out a big sigh. "What time is it now?"

The trunk glowed. "One thirty."

"Do you think Dad and Shoop miss us yet?"

"It's been over two hours since Rek dropped Craig at Toklat," Toni said as the trunk turned dark again. "I'm sure they're looking for us by now."

"Well, it won't be as hard to track down a missing helicopter as it is to find missing cubs," Buck said. "Plus, the rangers will have Rek's license plate number since he camped at Tek. Maybe there will be some roadblocks."

"I wonder where he's taking us," Toni said.

"I don't know, but I hope it's not too far. I know it's the least of our problems, but I have to pee."

"Me too," Toni said, and they both laughed a little.

It felt like a long time before the car slowed down

again. It made a left-hand turn but only sped up a little. The car lurched about, and rocks could be heard hitting the underside.

"I think we're on a dirt road now," Buck said as he and Toni bounced around inside the trunk. "What time is it?"

Buck looked at the compass as Toni looked at her watch. "Ten after two."

"We're going due east now," Buck said.

To their relief, they only bounced around for about ten minutes. Then the car slowed, stopped, and started slowly moving backward. As it moved in reverse, the car turned and seemed to be on smooth pavement for a few seconds before it stopped again. Then the steady beeping of an open car door could be heard over the sound of the running motor.

"I think we've backed into a driveway or something," Buck whispered.

"Yeah, and it sounds like Rek's gotten out," Toni said. "I bet we've gotten to wherever it is he's taking us."

"Hopefully, we'll be out of here soon," Buck said.

A few seconds later the car door slammed shut, and

the car slowly moved backward some more and stopped again. This time the motor turned off. The door opened and slammed shut again. Then nothing. Buck and Toni waited, but the trunk never opened.

"Where do you think we are?" Toni whispered in the dark.

"I don't know. I don't hear anything."

"I think he's gone," Toni said. "I think he's left us some-place."

"We have to get out of here," Buck said. "Move over. Maybe I can kick the backseat out."

Buck scooted around until his head was at the rear of the car, both feet flat on the back of the seat. He gave several forceful kicks. They made a lot of noise and the seat budged a little. He kicked again and again.

Suddenly a loud bang sounded from above them on the lid of the trunk, and they heard Rek yell, "Stop kicking at the seat! You're going to destroy my car."

Buck yelled the first thing he thought of. "I have to pee! You want me to pee all over your trunk?"

Instantly the trunk opened. Glaring lights hurt their

eyes as they looked up at Rek looking down at them, bear spray in his hand.

"I have to pee too," Toni said.

"Okay, you first, missy. Bucko, you stay there and keep down," Rek said, aiming the bear spray at Buck's face. "The john's over there."

Buck saw Rek point back behind him as Toni climbed out of the trunk, but lying flat on his back, he couldn't see much else. All he could tell was they were in a tall metal building. He lay there, looking at the rafters and keeping his eye on Rek. Rek seemed anxious about something and kept looking at his watch.

Suddenly Rek looked up and yelled. "Stop nosing around and get back here!"

When Rek yelled, something else started making noise. It sounded like pigs squealing.

"Those are the cubs, aren't they?" Toni asked. "They're under that tarp!"

In a flash Rek moved away from the trunk and grabbed at her.

"Ouch, let go! You're hurting me!"

Buck realized too late that this was his chance. He started to scramble out of the trunk, but Rek was already back, standing over him. He had Toni by her hair and was pulling so hard, her head tilted at an angle.

"You're not going anywhere, Bucko!" Rek snarled. Pushing Buck back down, Rek slammed the trunk closed. Again Buck was in the dark.

"Let me out of here!" Buck yelled. "What are you doing with Toni?" He started kicking at the seat again, adding to the noise of the squealing cubs.

Rek slammed his hand down on the trunk. "If you don't want anything to happen to your friend, you'd better shut up!" he yelled, but his voice trailed away from the car. Buck quieted.

"Get in there," Buck heard Rek say, "and don't even think about coming out."

A door slammed, and then a few seconds later the trunk suddenly opened up again.

"Get out," Rek said, the bear spray aimed at Buck again. "And get all your stuff, too."

Buck grabbed Toni's backpack and camera bag as he

climbed out. Squinting in the bright light, he looked around. The car had backed halfway into a huge metal building, big enough for six Green Beasts. Three big garage doors were at the front. In the back corner were two regular doors, both shut. Against the wall near the doors were two crates, each holding a squealing grizzly cub, one dark, one golden. An orange tarp lay on the floor, beside the crates. Other than that, the building was empty.

"Where's Toni?" Buck demanded.

"She's where you're going." Rek pushed Buck toward the doors. "Get in there." He pulled open one of the doors, shoved Buck into a small room, and slammed the door again. The only thing in the room was an old desk. Toni was sitting on it.

"Are you okay?" she said.

"Yeah," Buck answered. He dumped Toni's backpack and camera bag onto the desk. "Are you?"

"He pulled my hair real hard," Toni said, rubbing her head. As she spoke, the bears continued to squeal. But then there was another sound, a scraping sound like something heavy was being dragged across the floor just outside the door. The scraping soon stopped, and a few seconds later they heard the continuous *beep-beep-beep* of a car door left open.

"Sounds like Rek is in the car," Toni said. "I wonder if he's going to leave."

"I don't know, but I think he's blocked the door," Buck said. "If he's sitting in the car, he won't be looking this way. I'll see if I can push the door open." He slowly turned the doorknob. At first the door didn't budge, but when he pushed at it with his shoulder, it opened about an inch.

"One of the bear crates is in front of it. But if we both push together, we'll probably be able to get the door open enough to get out."

"We better come up with a plan first," Toni said. "Too bad there's not a window in here. There's a little one in the bathroom, but it's too small to climb out of."

"Where's the bathroom?" Buck said.

"Behind that other door," Toni said.

"Figures," Buck said. "Have you looked in the desk? Maybe there's a phone or something."

"It's empty."

"Darn," Buck said. He sat down, leaning against the wall. Toni took the sketchbook from her backpack and sat down next to him. She opened to the page where Buck had written down the directions they were flying.

"Maybe we can figure out where we are," she said. "Sure wish we had a map."

Buck suddenly jumped up. "We do!" he almost shouted. He ran over to the desk and pulled out the topographic map that was tucked into the pocket of the camera bag. "We never used it when we went with Craig."

As he spread the map on the desk, Toni put her finger to her mouth. "Shhhhh."

"What?" Buck asked. "I don't hear anything."

"That's just it," Toni said. "The car isn't beeping, and the cubs have quit squealing. Do you think Rek tranquilized them?"

"I don't know. Maybe they're just sleeping, but let's figure out where we are. If we can get out of here, we'll know where to run."

The two of them studied the map.

"We flew northeast at thirty-eight degrees," Buck said. He put the compass on the map. "So here's where we crossed the highway, and Healy must be that town we flew over. But we went past that. I'm guessing we landed here, near Lignite." Buck pointed to the map.

"Then we drove south," Toni said, her finger following a highway. "Here's that town with all the gift shops just before the park entrance. The map says it's called Glitter Gulch. We turned left about an hour from there."

"So we must be on this road, right here."

"Shhh!" Toni said suddenly. "Listen! This time I do hear something!"

They were both quiet for a second.

"It's a motor running!" Toni exclaimed.

"Someone's outside!" Buck added. "And listen, the garage door is opening. Someone's driving in!"

Buck started yelling. Then, rushing to the door, he put his shoulder to it. The cubs started squealing again as Toni joined him. Pushing with all their might, the door slowly moved a couple of inches, but Rek's face was right there. The bear spray was pointed toward the opening.

"Keep your mouths shut," he said. Buck immediately pulled the door closed.

"Whoever that is, I think they're coming for the cubs," Buck whispered. "When you went to the bathroom, Rek kept looking at his watch like he was expecting somebody."

"Let's listen," Toni said. "We might learn something."

The two stood quietly by the door as the cubs squealed on the other side. The motor turned off, and the garage door closed. Then a vehicle door slammed shut. A female voice spoke out loudly over the noise of the bears.

"Rek, what have you done with those two children?" Romana's voice demanded.

"Ohh!" Toni gasped.

"I can't believe it!" Buck whispered. "It's the Rails!"

"They're part of this!" Toni whispered back. "And they know Rek!"

"They knew he kidnapped us too!" Buck said.

"They're in there." Rek's voice was right on the other side of the door.

"They'd better not be hurt," Romana said.

"They're fine. I couldn't just let them run around here, waiting for you to show up. Where have you been, anyway? You were supposed to leave Tek first thing this morning, but I saw you out walking around on the river-bed. That kid pointed you out."

"It sounded like Romana's truly concerned about us," Toni said. "What do you think we should do?"

"Let's yell and push open this door," Buck said. "Pretend we couldn't hear them and we don't know they're in on it. Pretend we're glad to see them. When this door opens, we have to run out fast, bear spray or no bear spray. We can't do anything locked in here."

"Okay," Toni said, "but we might need our things, and I'm not coming back in here after them."

"We had plenty of time until we had to move your car," Gerald was saying as Toni stuffed the map and her sketch-book into her backpack.

Buck grabbed the camera bag. "Ready?" he whispered.

Toni whispered back, "Ready!"

Buck and Toni started yelling as loud as they could. "Help us! We're in here!"

They pushed at the door. It slowly budged.

"Help us get out!" Buck yelled.

"Rek, push that crate out of the way," Gerald demanded.

As Buck and Toni pushed on the door, Rek pushed the crate away and the door suddenly flew open. Buck nearly fell to the ground, but Toni dashed out past the bear crates and looked across the garage. The Rails' RV was on the far side. A small trailer was attached to the back.

"Romana! Gerald!" Toni called out as if in surprise. "It's you! You found us!"

As Toni raced to Romana and put her arms around the woman, Buck regained his balance. He started to run, but Rek grabbed at his arm. Buck swung the camera bag at him as hard as he could and hit the man in the stomach. Rek stumbled backward, giving Buck time to run over and stand with Romana and Toni near the RV. Rek started after Buck, but Gerald stepped in his path.

"Leave the kids alone," he said, his voice hard and unyielding. "You've made enough of a mess already, and we're not adding assault to the list."

Toni was still hugging Romana.

"I was so scared," she said, ignoring that she'd heard what Gerald had said. "That guy kidnapped us!" Tears were running down her cheeks.

"You're okay now," Romana said, then she turned to Buck. "Oh, look at your head. We need to get that washed up."

"I can clean it up," Toni insisted. She held up her backpack. "I always carry bandages with me after what happened to my finger. Can we go in your RV?"

Rek and Gerald were arguing. Romana looked over to them and back at Toni.

"Of course, dear," Romana replied. "The door's not locked. I'll be right in, but I better go see what's going on with Gerald first."

Buck and Toni hurried around to the other side of the RV. Buck pulled out the RV's step and opened the door. As soon as they were inside, Toni locked the door behind them.

"Let me go to the john," Buck said, "and then we'll figure out our next steps."

Buck tossed the camera bag onto the couch, went into

the bathroom, and closed the door. Toni looked out the window. It looked like Romana, Gerald, and Rek were all arguing now. She slowly slid the window open just a crack. They were talking so loud, Toni could hear them plainly.

"You better not leave those two alone very long," Rek cautioned. "You can't trust them."

"*You're* the one we can't trust," Gerald said.

"What on earth were you doing anyway?" Romana asked. "Flying around with that ranger and then kidnapping the kids?"

"I fly for anybody who hires me, and the park service is one of them. I was just making a little extra dough. I didn't know those brats would be coming."

"But kidnapping? You could have just taken the kids back to Tek," Gerald said.

"No, I couldn't. Buck recognized me."

"He wouldn't have recognized you if you hadn't been so stupid on the bus," Romana said. "Kicking her hand like that. What'd you do that for?"

"She got in my way."

When Buck came out of the bathroom, Toni was sitting on her knees on the couch, holding the camera up to a slightly open window.

"A little covert coverage," she whispered to him. "And they're talking so loud, I don't need the shotgun mic." Buck gave Toni the thumbs-up and joined her on the couch.

"So where's the money?" Rek was saying.

"I'm not paying you a cent," Gerald said. "All I hired you for was to fly those cubs out and keep them safe for a couple of days. Kidnapping wasn't part of the deal. I figure it's worth your paycheck for me to figure out what to do with those kids."

"Oh no, that's not the way it's going to happen. You're not leaving here with those cubs without paying me," Rek argued. "I did everything you wanted. Those cubs are right here like I said they would be."

"I want to take a look at them," Gerald said. "Make sure you haven't hurt them."

"I'm going to check on those kids first," Rek said. "I know they're up to something."

He started toward the RV, but this time Romana stepped in front of him.

"You've scared them enough," she said. "I'll check on them."

Rek and Gerald hurried toward the crates, and Romana headed toward the RV. Toni quickly shut off the camera and put it back into the bag.

"We've got to keep up the act," Buck said, "until we can come up with a good plan."

Buck raced to unlock the door as Toni slid the window closed. Then they sat side by side on the couch, both tense again.

"Are you two okay?" Romana asked when she opened the door. Her voice sounded concerned, but as she stepped inside, her eyes weren't on Buck and Toni. She was looking out the window, toward the crates.

"We're fine," Buck said. "Just a little shook-up."

"Can we stay in here?" Toni said. "I don't want to be near Rek."

"I don't blame you," Romana said, but she seemed distracted by whatever was going on between Gerald and

Rek. "But I need to get back out there. If you're hungry, there's peanut butter and jelly in the cupboard. I won't be long."

"That sounds great," Buck said, playing along. "We haven't had anything to eat since breakfast."

As Romana left the camper, Buck and Toni let out sighs of relief. Buck looked around. Like most campers, everything was tightly stored away while traveling.

"Let's see if we can find their phone," Buck said. "Maybe we can get a signal here."

Toni started going through the kitchen drawers as Buck went into the bedroom. Romana's red fleece lay rumpled on the bed, and Gerald's backpack sat on the floor, leaning against the closet door.

Maybe he has a phone in his backpack, Buck thought. He hurried over, flipped open the top flap, and looked inside.

"Holy cow!" he said, and raced to the door, almost running into Toni, who was charging into the bedroom.

"Look what I found!" both of them exclaimed at the same time.

TAKE 17:

"DON'T BE CAUGHT OFF GUARD. BEAR ATTACKS ARE LIGHTNING FAST!"

Toni held up a cell phone. "This was in a kitchen drawer!"

"Yeah, well, look at this!" Buck said, going over to the backpack. Keeping his back toward Toni, he reached in, pulled something out, and turned around.

"The sheep horn!" Toni exclaimed.

"Yeah, not only were they in on stealing the cubs, but they tricked us into hiking with them too! Just so they could take the horn!"

"Gerald wasn't making a nature call," Toni said. "He was getting rid of us so he could hide the horn in his backpack."

As she was talking, Toni turned on the phone. "Great," she said, tossing the phone onto the bed. "No signal."

"Gerald said they could get TV, Internet, cell phone, everything, remember?" Buck said.

He put the sheep horn on the bed, pushed the backpack out of the way, and opened the closet door. "All I have to do is turn a crank in here."

As he pushed the clothes aside, his hand hit something hard. Buck pulled the clothes away and looked in.

"You're not going to believe this!"

"Rek's case!" Toni said as Buck pulled a long black case marked with a big scratch from the closet. He set it on the bed near the sheep horn, and they sat down, the case between them.

"We finally get to see what's in it," Buck said. He flipped up the clasps and opened the lid.

"Whoa!"

Inside lay a disassembled rifle and two darts. There were empty spaces for three more darts. Buck stared at the gun, his mind rapidly putting the pieces together.

"I've got it," he said so suddenly that Toni jumped. He

pointed to the bed behind Toni. "It wasn't a red backpack. It was that! That's what threw us off!"

Toni looked to see what Buck was pointing at.

"Romana's fleece!" she exclaimed. "It was the Rails who were out in the tundra during the moose shot!"

"Exactly!" Buck said. "Rek camped next to them so he could bring them the gun and they could make their plans."

"And the helicopter I heard was Rek waiting up on the flat," Toni added. "As soon as we were gone, the Rails tranquilized the bears."

"That's right!" Buck said. "After the tranquilizers took effect, Rek flew down and got the cubs. The next-to-last bus had gone by, so they knew they had an hour to do it."

"That's why Gerald had such a big backpack! All the Rails had to do then was put the gun back in the case, stuff the case in the backpack, and walk out to the road to take the last green bus back to Tek. No one would suspect a thing. It would just look like they had been hiking."

"It makes perfect sense!" Buck said as he closed the case and snapped the latches shut.

"And things were going just fine until you two came nosing along!" Rek's vicious voice snarled.

Buck and Toni looked up. Rek stood in the bedroom doorway. In one hand was a roll of duct tape. In the other a canister of bear spray, his finger on the trigger.

"Thought you were pretty smart, didn't you? But you're not even smart enough to lock the door behind you." Rek tossed the duct tape onto the bed then continued talking. "So what to do with you. That's my problem. Slide that case over here, Bucko. And don't try anything, or Toni will get a shot of this." Rek turned the bear spray toward Toni.

As Rek spoke, Buck's mind was racing. *There are two more darts,* he thought. *One for me and one for Toni. I can't let Rek get that gun!*

The case was lying on its side, the two latches facing Buck, out of Rek's sight. Not moving his eyes from Rek, Buck slowly turned the combination dial beside one of the latches with his thumb, locking the case. Then with one hand, he slowly slid the case across the bed, but not toward Rek. He pushed it to the opposite side of the bed, out of Rek's reach. As he did so, Buck's other hand tightened around the sheep horn.

"Don't play games with me," Rek said. "Push it here." But when Buck remained still, Rek moved away from the doorway to grab the case. Keeping his eyes on Buck, Rek flipped one latch. It snapped open. Then Rek's hand went to the other latch. His thumb pushed on it, but nothing happened. Rek pushed on it again. When it didn't flip open, he looked down. Buck was ready for his chance this time. In one fast motion he hurled the sheep horn at Rek. The horn hit Rek in the chest, catching him off guard just long enough for Buck to lunge for the bear spray. He knocked it out of Rek's hand. It flew across the room and landed by the door. As Buck scrambled to get to it, Rek swung around, his hand in a fist aiming toward Buck's head. Toni instantly grabbed the case and swung it with all her might. The case hit Rek's arm midswing. There was an audible snap, and Rek doubled over in pain.

"You broke my arm!" he yelled. Rek looked like an angry bear ready to attack, but as Buck grabbed the bear spray, Toni held up the case.

"Sit down," she ordered, "or I'll hit you again."

Swearing, Rek sat down, cradling his arm.

"Shut up, Reko," Buck said, aiming the bear spray at him.

It was suddenly very quiet. Too quiet.

"Where are the Rails?" Buck asked. He quickly glanced out the window. "You probably wish you hadn't done that, Reko, old boy," Buck said sarcastically. "They might have come to your rescue and you'd be driving away with your money instead of sitting here with a broken arm."

Toni looked out the window too. Romana and Gerald sat on the garage floor near the crates. Their wrists and ankles were wrapped together with duct tape, and tape was across their mouths, too.

Toni picked up the duct tape and tore off a long piece. Staying out of Rek's reach, she stuck the end of it on the edge of the bed.

"Wrap that around your ankles," she said. When Rek didn't move, Toni lifted the black case threateningly. "Now!"

Rek scooted over until he could reach the tape. Using one hand, he clumsily wrapped his ankles together. As

Buck stood guard over Rek, Toni cranked up the satellite dish.

Soon she was on the phone, giving the police directions to the garage.

TAKE 18:

"DENALI NATIONAL PARK AND PRESERVE WAS ORIGINALLY ESTABLISHED TO PROTECT DALL SHEEP, BUT MOST PEOPLE COME HOPING TO SEE GRIZZLIES AND THE GREAT ONE."

SATURDAY, AUGUST 17

Saturday morning broke bright and clear. Buck and Toni had sat around the campsite all day Friday, answering questions from both the rangers and the police. The cubs had been taken to a vet to be checked out. Now Shoop sat in the front seat of the truck with Craig. Dad, Buck, and Toni were in back. Out across the tundra, a huge blond grizzly grazed on blueberries. She didn't even look up at the truck. Shoop pulled out the camera. Toni held the shotgun mic out the window.

"I can hear the chopper coming," she said. Buck looked

toward the sky but saw nothing.

Craig and Buck got out of the truck. Craig opened the tailgate and pulled out some cones with AREA CLOSED—BEAR DANGER signs on them. Buck helped set them along the side of the road. Then he stood beside one of the cones, looking at the distant grizzly.

Craig went back to the truck and pulled out a black case. Opening it, he took out his rifle, put a tranquilizer dart in it, and returned to stand by the cone next to Buck. As Shoop aimed the camera, Craig took off the safety, aimed, and shot. The grizzly stiffened, stood up, looked at Buck, and growled. It dropped back to its feet, took a few wobbly steps, stumbled over some alder bushes, and collapsed onto the ground.

Buck turned to look at the camera. Its red light was still on. "It will take about five minutes before she's fully out," he said. The light went off, and they waited.

When they heard the noise of a chopper's blades, the camera light went back on. Soon a helicopter flew over the mountain. Two crates swung from a cable below the chopper. It hovered above the tranquilized grizzly and then slowly came down until the crates touched the ground beside her.

"Come on," Craig said to Buck. "And you too, Toni. You both need to help me." Toni climbed out of the truck, and the three of them hurried over to the crates. Shoop and Dad followed with the camera and mic.

They unhooked the crates from the cable. Then, with the cable dangling, the chopper flew higher in the air until its blades no longer stirred up the dust around them.

"The vet said they were fine, just a little dehydrated," Craig said as he opened the crates. "The cubs and their mother will all wake up about the same time and won't even remember what's happened to them. They'll just go back to eating blueberries, getting ready for winter."

Craig and Buck pulled the golden cub out of the first crate. Toni helped Craig pull out the darker cub. Then the helicopter came back down. Craig hooked the empty crates up to the cable, and they all watched as the helicopter flew away.

"We need to leave now so the bears can wake up undisturbed," Craig said. They silently walked back across the tundra as the morning's first green bus drove past the cones, slowing down but not stopping.

. Leaving the cones along the road, they piled into Craig's truck and drove up and over the hill, past the Stony Dome overlook, and down the hairpin turns. Then Craig pulled to the side of the road and parked beside another ranger truck. K'eyush was waiting inside.

Buck climbed into Craig's truck bed. When he jumped out, he was holding the Dall sheep horn. He showed it to K'eyush, then put it into a backpack and hoisted it to his shoulders.

"I shouldn't have told anybody about the horn," Toni said as they started walking across the valley toward the creek.

"It's my fault too. I led Romana and Gerald straight to it," said Buck.

"No," Craig said. "It's Rek's, Romana's, and Gerald's fault. Rek wanted money and didn't care how he got it. Romana and Gerald wanted things that were not theirs."

"This horn and those bears belong here," K'eyush added in her quiet rhythmic voice. "We are only their fosters and protectors, not their owners."

The six continued walking through the valley toward the knobby mountains that looked like knuckles on a fist. They followed the creek, and when the walls closed in like a canyon, they climbed the embankment. They went higher, where the alders gave way to the short spongy tundra, and still higher, until they reached a point where the mountain dropped all the way around them. They continued on, around a rock pile, over a rise, and down a steep slope to a flat with two parallel lines in the tundra. Then they climbed halfway up another slope before skirting the side of the mountain. When they got to the rockslide, Shoop turned on the camera. Everybody stayed back, waiting for Buck to pull the sheep horn from his backpack and carry it to the rockslide. But Buck didn't do that. With a grin on his face, he reached into his backpack, but he pulled something else out and tossed it to Toni. Toni caught an official *Wild World of Buck Bray* shirt and gave Buck a puzzled look.

"You have to look official," Buck said. Toni smiled and slipped on the shirt, but she hung back.

"Come on. We're doing this together," Buck said. "We're a team, aren't we?"

As the red light glowed on Shoop's camera, Buck and Toni carried the Dall sheep horn to the edge of the rockslide. And, as they placed the gracefully curved horn on the rocks, Denali, the Great One, watched.

GLOSSARY

BENCH: A long, narrow strip of level land that is surrounded by steeper slopes both above and below it.

BOAR: A male grizzly bear.

BRAIDED RIVER: A river with small, relatively shallow channels of water that divide and then recombine many times, making the water channels look like the strands of a braid woven with the gravel bars and islands that separate them.

CACHE (PRONOUNCED "CASH"): A hiding place to store things for a short while. Animals will make a food cache to hide food to eat at a later time.

CAIRN: Rocks purposely mounded to mark a specific place or show the direction of a trail.

CALF: A young caribou or young moose.

CARCASS: The remains of a dead animal.

CLIFF FACE: The vertical (or up and down) side of a cliff.

COW: A female caribou or female moose.

DRAW: The low land of a V that is formed when two hillsides come together.

GRAVEL BAR: Rocks (as well as mud, sand, and other sediments) that have been forced by the actions of the water to form long ridges of "solid ground." Sometimes gravel bars are along the banks of rivers, sometimes they are surrounded by water, like islands.

KNIFE-EDGE: The long but extremely narrow ridge that is formed at the top of where two very steep mountain slopes meet.

KNOLL: Small rounded hill.

LICHEN: A plantlike living organism made of both algae and fungus that help each other to live. The algae produces food and the fungus gathers water. Lichen look like crusty blotches on the surface of rocks and trees and may be orange, red, yellow, green, or brown.

MUDFLAT: Flat, exposed areas of mud left uncovered when the water usually covering it has drained away.

RACK: Another name for antlers.

RAVINE: A deep, narrow, steep-sided valley or gorge that is usually created by running water. It is similar to a canyon but smaller.

RUT: The fall breeding season for moose and caribou. Often these animals display unpredictable behavior and are more dangerous during this time.

SHALE: A kind of soft rock made of hardened clay that breaks easily into thin flat pieces.

SOAPBERRIES: A type of edible but very bitter red berry that grows on small shrubs in the Alaskan wilderness.

SOW: A female grizzly bear.

THICKET: A thick group of small shrubs or trees that grow closely together.

TUNDRA: Treeless Arctic lands where the ground below the topsoil is frozen year-round. It is covered with low-lying plant life such as grasses, small bushes, mosses, and lichen. Sometimes the tundra plant-life is referred to as "tundra." Also, mountain areas above timberline are often referred to as mountain tundra.

JUDY YOUNG

Judy Young is the award-winning author of more than twenty children's books, including the middle-grade novel *Promise* and the picture book *A Pet for Miss Wright*, which was read by LeVar Burton in a Reading Rainbow Story Time Video for National Reading Month. An avid outdoors person, Judy spent four months camping, hiking, and fishing in northwestern Canada and Alaska while doing research for *The Missing Grizzly Cubs*. Staying ten days in Denali National Park and Preserve, she encountered moose, caribou, Dall sheep, and grizzlies. Judy resides with her husband, Ross, in the mountains near Mink Creek, Idaho, where any day she may see deer, elk, moose, black bears, and mountain lions. For a behind-the-story adventure, see Buck Bray's Wild World Scrapbook on Judy's website, www.judyyoungpoetry.com.